"Master, your wish is my command."

"Er, okay. Well, Lily, we need to talk." Ethan tugged at his tie and scanned the condo, now full of decorative objects and brightly colored pillows.

Lily quickly approached him and began loosening the knot at his throat. Her scent drifted to him and he closed his eyes and breathed it in. "What is that perfume?"

"Bergamot, lavender and sandalwood," she said as she slowly slid his tie away and began undoing his shirt buttons. "Do you like it?"

He breathed in again. "Yeah."

She smiled. "Come, rest yourself." Taking him by the hand, she led him to the sofa. Rather than sitting beside him, she stood before him and twirled once. "Does Master like my outfit?"

How could he not? It was a classic harem-girl costume. "Sure, but—"

"Would Master like his slave to dance?"

Slave? "Yes," he heard himself answer as if from far away. She was doing it again...leading him down the rabbit hole, into her fantasy world. He gave up the fight and followed.

Blaze

Dear Reader,

Have you ever met someone so quirky and free-spirited that they instantly made you feel better about life? I have. I've known her a long time and have always thought she'd make a great character in a book. With a few changes to protect her innocence, of course. <wink> But the essence is there. Her joy. Her tolerance for all our imperfections and differences. And her love of life. Throw in a little belly dancing, and a well-used deck of tarot cards, and you've got Lily.

Then, when Lieutenant Colonel Ethan Grady showed up as Cole's friend in *Let It Ride*, I just knew that free-spirited character would be the perfect yin to his yang. This repressed air force fighter pilot has met his match in Lily.

We're back at Nellis Air Force base. Home of the Air Base Defense School, where an elite team of fighter pilots teach daring air-combat maneuvers. Oh, those men and their uniforms. With Sin City only a few miles away, anything can happen. And in a Harlequin Blaze novel, you know it's going to be sizzling hot.

I was so thrilled to hear from readers who enjoyed *Let It Ride* and hope you love this story just as much (and yes, Mitch and Alex are at it again, and yes, they will be getting their own story, coming soon). Please drop me a note and check out information on my next Harlequin Blaze book at www.jillianburns.com.

Enjoy!

Jillian Burns

Jillian Burns

SEDUCE AND RESCUE

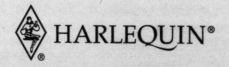

HARLEQUIN®

TORONTO • NEW YORK • LONDON
AMSTERDAM • PARIS • SYDNEY • HAMBURG
STOCKHOLM • ATHENS • TOKYO • MILAN • MADRID
PRAGUE • WARSAW • BUDAPEST • AUCKLAND

Recycling programs
for this product may
not exist in your area.

ISBN-13: 978-0-373-79576-5

SEDUCE AND RESCUE

Printed in U.S.A.

ABOUT THE AUTHOR

Jillian Burns has always read romance, and spent her teens immersed in the worlds of Jane Eyre and Elizabeth Bennett. She lives in Texas with her husband of twenty years and their three active kids. Jillian likes to think her emotional nature—sometimes referred to as *moodiness*—has found the perfect outlet in writing stories filled with passion and romance. She believes romance novels have the power to change lives with their message of eternal love and hope.

Books by Jillian Burns

HARLEQUIN BLAZE
466—LET IT RIDE

Don't miss any of our special offers. Write to us at the following address for information on our newest releases.

Harlequin Reader Service
U.S.: 3010 Walden Ave., P.O. Box 1325, Buffalo, NY 14269
Canadian: P.O. Box 609, Fort Erie, Ont. L2A 5X3

I had a lot of inspiration for this book and am so lucky to have wonderful friends and family from whom I gather information. Huge thanks to Susan Grant, military pilot and author extraordinaire, who was so gracious to answer all my air force questions. To sis, Mindy, for the belly-dancing inspiration, and to dear friend Von for the tarot-card lessons and guidance in all things enlightened.

And especially to Melody. You inspired Lily long before I knew she was Lily.

And, as always, thank you to my two superhero critique partners, Pam and Linda, who always go above and beyond. And to my brilliant editor, Kathryn.

1

How the heck had he gotten himself into this situation?

Lieutenant Colonel Ethan Grady clenched his fists as he studied the chaotic mess inside the herb shop located a few blocks off the Vegas strip.

He'd lost a bet, that's how.

And now he had to get a massage from some old gypsy lady who kept voodoo doodads hanging from the ceiling and bottles of smelly herbs and oils crammed on wall-to-wall shelves. Whatever space wasn't filled with bottles held candles or plants or…cats.

Ethan looked down at a long-haired black cat winding its way around his leg, and his fists tightened. Now he'd have cat fur on his BDUs.

"Well, buddy." His fellow airman, Captain Mitch McCabe, shot him an evil grin as he slapped him on the back. "Time to pay up."

"And you never know," his buddy Jackson, who'd won

the bet, added. "You may like it so much you become a regular."

Ethan scowled. Not in this lifetime.

He never gambled. But ever since he'd learned of Jackson's close call with death, something inside Ethan just...felt different. Besides, he'd wanted Jackson's fifty-year-old bottle of Scotch. And the bet had looked like a sure thing. Who'd have thought the Keno girl would give in to Jackson when she'd turned down every other airman within a hundred-mile radius?

Women were illogical.

"Namaste." A high, sweet voice floated to him from the back of the small shop. "I'm Lily."

Ethan shook his boot in an attempt to dissuade the black cat from circling his ankles, and looked up into huge Caribbean-blue eyes as the girl straightened from a bow, her palms still together. Untamed strawberry curls framed a pixie face with an upturned nose. Tiny dimples added the perfect touch to a creamy complexion as she flashed a ready smile from a beautiful mouth.

The neon sign out front read Lily's. But this was no old gypsy.

The redhead's smile faded and her curved brows crinkled into a frown. She tilted her head and moved closer. Too close. "Oh, my." For a minute Ethan thought she was going to cry. "Your aura is black. So dull, so... heavy." Her arms rose and she held up her hands, one over his stomach and the other over his crotch.

She squeezed her eyes shut, then opened them to stare into his again. "Several of your chakras are completely blocked. This makes your chi rough and chaotic." Her eyes closed and her head fell back as she flattened her palms against his chest and moved them down and around.

The instant she touched him his body sizzled and stirred. Ethan grabbed her wrists, removed her hands and stepped back.

McCabe chuckled and exchanged stupid grins with Jackson. "Sounds like Grady's got himself a real unhealthy chi, there. Lily, maybe you can unstick that poker up his a—"

"Shut it, McCabe." Ethan threw him his fiercest glare.

Jackson stepped between them. "Our friend here has an appointment for a massage."

The hippie swept her attention back to Ethan, her eyes even wider. "You're Mitch's friend. Another air force pilot. So that's what the cards were trying to tell me."

Cards? Enough of this new age crap. "Let's get this over with."

"Lieutenant Colonel…Grady, isn't it?" She put her finger to her tiny chin and began studying his body as she circled him.

Ethan purposely unclenched his fists and tried to relax. But he couldn't do it with her gaze burning into him. Then he felt her hands touch his shoulders, and he flinched. She made a *hmm* sound and then crooned an *oooh* as her hands moved down his arms. Ethan stifled a shiver.

"This will take more than a massage." Her serious tone was at odds with her soft high voice.

"Oh, he wants to take yoga lessons, too," Jackson interjected.

"Don't you have somewhere to be?" Ethan growled.

"All right, all right. I think you're in good hands." Jackson turned to the herb lady. "Take care of our buddy, ma'am."

"Do you have a girlfriend, Lieutenant Colonel? A lover?" She moved around in front of him and narrowed her eyes.

"He's as free as a cocktail in a casino, sweetheart," McCabe said, and winked at her.

"You're done here, McCabe." Ethan crossed his arms and jerked his head toward the exit.

The redhead dimpled at McCabe and then gestured to a doorway covered by hanging beads. "This way, Lieutenant Colonel."

Ethan waited until the shop door had shut behind Jackson and McCabe, and then followed her through the doorway, careful to hold the strings of beads out of his way.

He stopped short inside the back room. It was cramped and lit only with more burning candles. His nose was assaulted by a sweet yet spicy scent. A red-and-yellow tie-dyed scarf was draped over the only window. A miniature fountain surrounded by river rocks and plants gurgled in the corner. But the main feature in the center of the room was the massage table. He'd rather face combat than lie on that thing.

"Just strip down to whatever you're comfortable in." She turned to leave the room.

"I'm comfortable now."

She laughed, a light tinkling sound, and swiveled to smile at him. Her brows rose with skepticism and he clenched his teeth together.

"Why is that funny?"

"I don't think you've been 'comfortable' in years. Perhaps decades."

"Look, you don't know me, so you can stop with the woo-woo weirdo act and just get on with it."

She blinked up at him, her full lips pouting, and he felt as if he'd just kicked a puppy.

"I guess I shouldn't be surprised at your rudeness, with an aura like that," she said, shaking her head. "Who wouldn't be grumpy with their chi in such a state? I need to find just the right aroma for you." She spun and left the room.

Ethan could hear her light voice out front, chattering, he assumed, to herself. "Let's see…patchouli? No, no. Too stimulating. Maybe lavender. No, too weak. Something powerful, yet relaxing."

Rude? Grumpy? She was right. He normally prided himself on his even-keeled nature. And his honorable treatment of females. He'd let this whole situation get under his skin.

Stop being such a wuss. He'd spent more than half his life in the air force. He'd faced down enemy bombers in the first Gulf War at the tender age of twenty-three. Witnessed kids younger than him shot, or blown up in land mines.

He drew in a deep breath, and with it, regained control. This would be over in an hour, tops. He could endure anything for an hour. Then he'd carry on with life as usual.

"Oh, you're still dressed."

Ethan blinked at the woman in her flowing, rainbow-striped robe. She'd tied back her hair, and held a small, strangely shaped bottle filled with clear liquid. "Have you changed your mind?"

"No."

She put her finger to her chin again, staring at him. "Have you ever had a massage before?"

"No."

"Never? Oooh, a massage virgin." She grinned and her dimples teased his libido. And for some weird reason, so did the word *virgin*. "You're going to love it," she continued, clasping the bottle to her stomach with both hands. "It's so relaxing, and I can tell by the set of your shoulders how tense you are. I've had only one other massage virgin, and she was…"

Ethan stopped listening. No, he wasn't going to love it. He didn't want to be touched. He didn't like physical contact. Even when… He thought back to the arrangement he'd had with a lady he'd met in town. Every Friday night he would pick her up, take her to dinner, then go back to her place. Excessive touching had never been part of the deal. She hadn't voiced any objections. Not in two years. But then she had canceled their standing date without a qualm.

"Okay, then, remove everything except your undershorts, get on the table and lie on your stomach." Lily peeled the robe off her shoulders, spun and hung it on the tail of a brass kitty cat wall hook.

Ethan barely contained his slack-jawed reaction. The robe had hidden a trim figure in cutoff shorts and a tight tank top. Gorgeous legs. Tiny waist. Slim hips. Good-sized…she wasn't wearing a bra.

And he had to strip down to his skivvies.

She set the bottle on the windowsill and headed out front again. "Call me when you're ready."

Heat surged through his body. Every part. Dragging his thoughts away from the woman's breasts, Ethan pictured the icy winter days of his childhood in South Dakota. He sat on a chair by the door to pull off his boots and socks, and envisioned himself at Thule Air Base in Greenland staring at the arctic tundra. As he unbuttoned his uniform shirt, pulled it off one sleeve at a time and folded it carefully, he remembered the freezing snow on the Afghan mountaintops. Closing his eyes, he unzipped his camo pants, stepped out of them and folded them just as neatly.

"Are you ready back there, Lieutenant Colonel Grady?"

Ethan almost snarled. She'd broken his concentration. He snapped off his undershirt, wrapped a towel over his boxer briefs and lay down on his stomach.

Beads tinkled as she entered the room. "Close your eyes and take a deep, slow breath."

Ethan gritted his teeth and complied.

With a click the sound of waves crashing against a shore filled the room. "To achieve Zen, one must be in total peace with oneself and nature." Her warm, oil-soaked hands landed on his shoulders, and he instantly stiffened. But then she began a soft caress along either side of his neck, while her thumbs slid up his nape into his hairline.

He inhaled again and the light scent of coconut aroused his senses. The arctic was gone, replaced with a balmy beach, palm trees and a bikini-clad—

Her. The wacky herb lady. Lily.

He was picturing her in a bikini. In an instant his make-believe self had joined her on the sand and his hands were gripping her waist, then sliding up—

Discipline, Grady.

"Whoa. What happened? You were just starting to relax when your shoulders tightened up again." Her fingers massaged his temples in slow circles, then combed through his hair to knead his scalp. "Empty your mind of thoughts," she said in a low voice. "Negative thoughts create negative energy. Breathe in slowly, deeply. Then release impurities as you exhale."

Since he was here and committed to this, he might as well try to gain some benefit from it. He blew out the breath he'd been holding, and tried to concentrate on fighting his intense aversion to physical contact.

"That's it, Ethan. Very good." The praise lightened

something inside him. Her voice seemed to be whispering right into his soul, its soft entreaty arousing.

With his eyes closed, his other senses sharpened. The evocative scent of coconut. The repetitive waves crashing and retreating. The touch of skin against skin. Her hands worked their way down his spine, stroking, rubbing, deep into his flesh. As she reached the small of his back, he felt her strokes change from the broader heel of her hand to pointed knuckles making quick circles.

Her knuckles worked their way up his back again and then she started massaging his shoulders, and down his arms, her fingers kneading the muscles. All the while she talked. "Feel your heart rate slow," she crooned. "Listen to each breath you take."

Her voice soothed him as she performed miracles on his feet and calves, spreading oil as she caressed up his thighs. Maybe there was something to this massage thing. He *was* feeling more relaxed….

Before he knew it, she had him turn over. When he raised his arms to clasp his hands beneath his head, he brushed her breast. A breast that wasn't covered with a bra. A breast that was the most perfect shape. And the nipple of which had hardened to a bead against his forearm. Suddenly, he realized he'd lost control of his arousal.

She froze. Time seemed suspended. All he could hear was her breathing, quick and ragged.

Ethan closed his eyes, barely stifling a groan. To his horror, his dick hardened even more.

No way she didn't notice his wood.

Surely this was a common physical reaction to a massage. Wasn't it?

Her hands resumed their caressing, working their way slowly down to his stomach and then on to the edge of the towel. When she moved to his thighs, she brushed against his out-of-control erection, and he jackknifed up and bolted off the table. But he lost his footing, stumbled into the windowsill and knocked over several candles. Flames instantly ignited the silk scarf.

After staring in disbelief for an instant, he turned to the woman. "Go get your fire extinguisher."

She blinked at the spreading flames. "I'm not sure… I don't think I have one."

"Don't have one? How could you…" Looking around, he grabbed the fountain and splashed water onto the fire, which had reached the shelves full of bottles of…*crap.* Of oil. The flames leaped higher. The cord from the fountain knocked over several bottles when he yanked it from the wall, and the water pushed the flames closer to the spilled oil. *Great.*

The fire popped and crackled. Smoke swirled thick and black in the tiny room. His eyes stung. He coughed and turned to tell Lily to get out and call 911, but she'd disappeared. *Good.* She was ahead of him. He probably only had time for one more chance before the fire engulfed the entire room, if not the premises.

Think, Grady! Oil fires. Baking soda. He needed something to smother it with. Of course. He headed back to the front room, grabbed up the largest potted plant, ripped out the plant and tried to get back in to dump the damp soil on the flames, but the fire had all but consumed the room.

One small planter of soil wouldn't even slow it down.

As he ran for the front door, Lily appeared in his path carrying the black cat, a tan-and-white guinea pig and a bird cage containing a plump white cockatoo. She thrust them into his arms, her face soot-coated but determined. "Take Ingrid, Scarlett and Bette. I've got to get Humphrey and Rhett." She spun on her heel, heading back into the fog of smoke.

What the hell?

"Wait." He set the birdcage down, tightened his hold on the squirming animals and lunged forward to block her way. "You're not going anywhere except out. *I'll* get Humphrey and Rhett." He handed her the cat and the guinea pig. "Who are Humphrey and Rhett?"

Her face crumpled even as she coughed. "Humphrey's my basset hound. He's old and almost blind, and I couldn't find him. He always sleeps in front of the TV, but he wasn't there." She pointed behind the counter to a set of stairs Ethan hadn't noticed before. "And Rhett's a big orange tabby. He won't come willingly."

"I'll find them. Now get out of here." More animals? Was she insane? Ethan took the stairs three at a time and opened the door into a relatively smoke-free one-room apartment. If he was lucky he had maybe two minutes before the fire burned through the ceiling.

Now, if he were a dog, where would he hide? Crossing the room in two strides, Ethan dropped to his knees beside the bed and lifted the bedcovers. Sure enough, the stupid mutt was lying sprawled on his side, as if he hadn't a care in the world.

Ethan swept the solid lump of dog into his arms, stopped to grab up an orange, hissing, scratching tabby, and then bolted down the stairs just as the ceiling snapped and a falling two-by-four cracked across his shoulder blades, knocking him to his knees. Pain shot down his spine and the room spun around him.

LILY HEARD THE CRACK of splintering wood. *Mother Earth, protect him.* She bit her thumbnail, shifting her weight from one bare foot to the other, her attention riveted on the doorway. But Lieutenant Colonel Grady wasn't coming out....

All she could see of the shop now were flames.

Mist had called 911, Sunny had taken Scarlett and Ingrid to her house, and Lily's other neighbors had gathered across the street from her shop to offer aid and to commiserate.

He just *had* to emerge unhurt.

The tarot had turned up the Tower, a card of radical transformation. In some cases it could mean the destruction of one's home. *Her home.* But she'd think about that later. Lieutenant Colonel Grady had to be okay. There'd been no indication of death or even injury in the cards.

The moment she'd seen Ethan Grady she'd known he was her next project. She was meant to help him. Just as she had been destined to be there for Theo. And the others who'd followed him. When she received a sign from the universe to help someone, she could no more ignore it than she could let one of her pets come to harm.

But how could she help this Ethan Grady if—

There he was! The lieutenant colonel came striding out of the wall of flames holding Rhett and Humphrey as if it were the most natural thing in the world for a man wearing only his undershorts to rescue an old hound dog and a spitting, fighting alley cat from a burning building.

Lily ran to him. "Thank you." She beamed at him as she took Humphrey. "Oh, Humphrey, were you scared, sweet pea?" She nuzzled the basset hound's neck, then turned to set him down on the grass. Mist relieved the man of Rhett, whose claws were dug deep into the poor lieutenant colonel's shoulder.

Immediately, Lily placed her hand on Ethan's arm. "Are you okay?"

Glaring at her, he stiffened beneath her touch, his spine straight, his jaw clenched. Sirens wailed in the distance as he cleared his throat. "How could you *not know* where your fire extinguisher is?"

Lily noted his accusing scowl. But she was saved from answering as he grabbed his ribs and bent over, coughing and hacking, his free hand propped on his knee.

Worried, she placed her palm on his back to rub, and noticed the red, swollen bump between his shoulder blades. He *had* been hurt.

She asked Sunny to get him a glass of water and an ice pack. Sunny nodded and headed back to her shop, but not before giving Lieutenant Colonel Grady's nearly naked form an appreciative once-over. A possessive tendril flared in Lily's belly, but she couldn't blame her friend.

The gorgeous man *was* standing in the street wearing nothing but his black boxer briefs and dog tags. His biceps were enormous; his body, though soot-covered, was a testament to nature's divine purpose. What female could look at those broad shoulders, that dusting of dark hair across sculpted pecs, and my oh, my, that impressive package, and *not* want to procreate with such a man? Hadn't *she* been tempted to stray where she never had before with a massage client?

Her gaze traveled up to his gray-green eyes, the color so at odds with his stern demeanor, but just as their stares met, he spun and began barking orders to the onlookers to pull out hoses from their yards and water down the neighboring buildings.

He took control of the entire crowd, commanding obedience from total strangers. And he did it wearing nothing but boxers. Such domineering behavior would normally be a turnoff for her, but that was exactly what was needed right now. With the drought and the winds, the fire could spread.

A fire truck rolled to a stop beside them and they were all ushered out of the way while huge hoses were unfolded and hooked up to a hydrant. Lily watched in anguish as the firemen contained the flames. Black smoke billowed into the sky and even before the blaze had been extinguished, she knew. There was no saving her shop. Everything was gone. The only place she'd ever been able to call her own, the fruits of Theo's legacy to her, lost in minutes.

A lump of bittersweet memories formed in her throat. Of Theo, so happy, placing the Cracker Jack ring on her left finger in the chapel on the Vegas strip. Of him waving goodbye from the airfield. Despite the grief and guilt, she'd honored his wish and used her survivor benefits to buy the shop. And she'd been happy here.

But fate was calling her toward a different path now.

She wiped at the tears and searched for Ethan Grady. A paramedic approached him with oxygen and a blanket. He wrapped the blanket around his waist, but waved off the oxygen, then stepped forward when a Las Vegas police officer approached him to take his statement.

Another officer questioned her. Without going into details, she explained that the candle had been accidentally knocked over. Every few minutes she glanced back at Ethan to smile in reassurance. This was meant to be. Somehow, this lonely lieutenant colonel's fate was entwined with hers for a short while along life's journey.

Eventually the policemen left, the firemen loaded up their equipment and the truck rolled off. The crowd dispersed, except for Lily's closest friends.

Though he didn't have room, Mist offered to take her in. Dear Mist, with his waist-length dreads and multiple piercings, eyed Ethan suspiciously. But when she told him about her reading with Sunny this morning, he seemed to relax. Sam and Simone had just returned from their bikers' rally in Reno, and Simone was deathly allergic to cat dander. Sunny, in her muumuu and wild silver hair, nodded reassuringly with a wink and a wiggle of her penciled-in eyebrows.

And Lieutenant Colonel Ethan Grady… Lily looked over at him, drinking in the firm line of his jaw, the hard glint in his eyes. Even wearing only underwear and a blanket he was formidable. *Could* she help him?

She'd been so young when she'd married Theo. Just out of high school. But even then she'd known she had a gift. She could sense things in people—whether they were hurting, and whether she could help heal them. Her talent might be unconventional, but she knew she'd made a difference in many lives. And wasn't that a person's ultimate goal in the universe? To help each other?

Now, it was Ethan's turn. The black fog of sadness surrounding him stirred something deep inside her. Oh, yes. He needed her.

Holding her stare with his own, Ethan straightened, as if preparing for battle, and closed the distance between them. His back must have been throbbing in pain, yet he showed no sign of it as he faced her. "Are you all right?"

"I'm fine. Thank you again for saving Humphrey and Rhett. I was so scared. That was the bravest thing anyone's ever done for me."

"That's one way to look at it." He glanced across the

street to the charred remains of her shop. "Do you have somewhere to stay tonight?"

She had the perfect place. If he only knew… "Ethan." She placed her hand on his arm, gentling him to her touch. "I believe this was a sign."

His mouth quirked in derision. "A sign that you should find another line of work?"

"No, not exactly. I believe karma brought you into my life for a reason."

His brows drew together. "Karma?" His tone was intimidating.

"Yes, you see, the universe is telling me I'm meant to help you."

"Please." He held up his hands as if to ward her off. "Don't help me."

"But you need me. And if I live with you for a short while I can bring your chi back into balance, unblock your—"

"Live with me?" His mouth tightened into a thin line and he stepped back. "Don't you have family—someone you can call?"

She was shaking her head before he'd even finished his questioning. "My only family is my mom, and she lives in San Diego."

"What about your friends here?" He gestured to the group surrounding her.

"Simone is allergic, Sunny has less square footage than my place and Mist has a pet clause in his lease."

Ethan shook his own head. "Look, ma'am. I realize this was partially my fault. Let me put you up in a hotel. Why don't you take—" Ethan reached for a nonexistent back pocket, then his mouth tightened and his jaw muscle ticked. "My wallet was inside." He eyed her empty arms. "And your purse, too, I guess."

"Oh, no. My purse is in my car."

"You keep your purse in your car?"

"Of course. I only need it when I'm going somewhere."

He blinked. "Fine. You pay for the hotel and I'll be glad to *reimburse* your expenses."

She couldn't help but laugh at that. "I can't bring Scarlett and Rhett, and Humphrey and—"

"Right," he interrupted. "No hotel." As he looked around at all the animals, a hint of panic settled into his expression.

She grinned, triumphant. Of course the cosmos wouldn't have taken away everything she owned without a reason. "You see? It's karma. And you can't argue with karma."

"Watch me," he grunted as he half turned away, looking like a man desperate to escape.

"Ethan," she said, bringing his attention back to her. She was starting to worry. Would he truly refuse her? She had to convince him. "I don't have anywhere else to go."

He made a noise that sounded like a low feral growl. Then he stared at the ground a moment until finally he let out a resigned breath. "I can't believe I'm going to do this." He spun on his heel and headed for a large black

SUV parked a block down the street. "You can follow in your car."

She motioned for her friends to bring the rest of her pets, picked up Bette's cage and followed.

But the lieutenant colonel stopped short at the door to his SUV. His keys were probably with his wallet in the pocket of his uniform pants, along with whatever else he carried. All of it incinerated now. Of course, the military officer was prepared. He reached under the chassis and pulled out a magnetic spare key box.

Silently directing Mist and Sunny to load her loved ones into her orange 1989 Toyota—affectionately known as The Pumpkin—parked in the alley, Lily rose up on her tiptoes to give Ethan a peck on the cheek. "Thank you."

He ground his teeth, took Bette's birdcage from her and placed it in his backseat. "This is just for a couple of days, until we can sort this mess out."

A couple of days? Oh, she had a feeling this project would take a bit longer than that.

2

LILY OPENED HER EYES slowly and rolled to her back. It wasn't quite dawn, but enough light filtered through the builder-grade blinds to remind her where she was. Bare beige walls. Plain white ceiling fan. She was in Ethan's bedroom. Where he'd insisted she sleep last night.

Memories of the fire slammed into her psyche and a pang of grief tightened her throat. Her shop, her home, everything. Gone.

She rolled back over and curled into a ball, acknowledging the ache in her stomach, letting the pain of loss seep into her bones. This was exactly how she'd felt after receiving word that Theo had been killed in Iraq. She'd known before he shipped out that something bad would happen to him. Had tried to warn him. And in the end, she'd given in and married him, hoping that would stop the bad feeling in her gut and let him face war with a positive energy surrounding him. He'd loved her so much, he'd deserved that, at least.

And thinking of positive energy… Acknowledging

pain was one thing. Wallowing in self-pity would only produce negative vibes. She sat up, wiped at the tears on her cheeks and looked around the room.

The sleek black, king-size bed was ultracomfortable, but the matching contemporary-style dresser was the only other furniture in the sterile room. The only other thing, period. This room—the entire condo—reflected Ethan's life. Bland. Empty.

But today she would begin to change all that.

She had to believe that the devastation last night had happened for a reason. Ethan needed her here.

Drawing in a deep, cleansing breath she folded her legs and placed her hands palm up on her knees. As she exhaled she blew out all negative thoughts, closed her eyes and cleared her mind.

Before she could begin meditating Humphrey howled and scratched at the door. Lily opened her eyes to find her black-and-tan basset hound glaring at her expectantly. She sprang off the bed, picked up the cereal bowl that was his makeshift water bowl, and padded into the living area to let him out.

Just off the kitchen was a door that led out to the tiny, fenced-in grassy area. Hardly a yard. But at least there were no stairs for Humphrey to have to limp down, as there were at her place. "Nooo, no mean ol' stairs for Humphrey," she sang as the dog waddled outside. She'd take him for a walk this evening.

The kitchen was all black granite and stainless appliances. Functional. Uncluttered. In the stark main room there was more of the same. The dark wood floors were bare. There was a black leather couch—more like a black hole sucking up all the positive energy in the room—a monster-size black television and a silver floor lamp. That was it. No plants, no tables, nothing of color. And no pictures of friends or family, either. It was going to take some shopping to fix the feng shui in Ethan's condo.

She was tempted to peek in and see if he was still sleeping in the spare room, crammed between a weight machine and a punching bag. The futon couldn't be very comfortable for someone his size, but he wouldn't even listen to her protests last night, stubborn man.

What would it take to move him from the futon back to his bed to unblock his sacral chakra?

With a shrug, Lily decided to think about that later. She closed her eyes, pressed her palms together and raised them above her head, and rose up on the balls of her feet: salutation to the sun.

She bent at the waist and flattened her hands on the floor, touching her forehead to her knees. Closing her eyes, she concentrated on her breathing. She walked her feet back into the downward facing dog position, stretching out her spine. She held the position a moment, but the T-shirt she'd borrowed last night bunched around her shoulders and fell in her face. Without thinking, she pulled it off and then resumed the pose.

But what if Ethan woke up and came in here? She wasn't ashamed of her body, but she wasn't an exhibitionist, either. Well, she'd hear the doorknob turn and could yank the shirt back on before he got down the hall.

With a click the dead bolt turned and the front door whooshed open. "What the—"

Lily looked up just as Ethan slammed the door closed and spun to turn his back to her. She grabbed the shirt as she straightened, and held it in front of her. "*Namaste,* Ethan." Her heartbeat raced and her breathing stuttered. She'd always been comfortable with her sexuality, but there was an energy that crackled between her and this remote man. She'd felt it as soon as he'd walked into her shop.

"Would you please put some clothes on?" Ethan growled through his teeth. He was wearing athletic shorts and a T-shirt with a sweat stain clinging to the middle of his back. His black, military short hair was wet also. He'd been running. Before dawn.

Something visceral pumped through her as she breathed in the energy of this large, hard-muscled man. His glutes were taut. His scent was musky. Her body answered the call of man to woman.

"I always practice yoga before work," she said, sticking her head through the T-shirt and shoving her arms through the sleeves. "But I lost my leotard along with the rest of my clothes."

He gave a wary glance behind him, then turned to face her.

"Did your friend mean it when he said you wanted to learn?" Lily asked. "During yoga you commune with your body and strengthen your mind. It's a spiritual quest for unity and illumination."

"Ma'am?" He raised his left wrist to look at a

serviceable watch on a leather band. "I have to be at the base in a half hour."

"On a Saturday? And please call me Lily."

He glanced down and gestured loosely at the lower half of her body. "Don't you at least wear— Never mind." Taking a step, he almost tripped over Ingrid, who circled his leg, purring and rubbing her head against him. With an expression of annoyance, he gently pushed her away with his running shoe before striding into the kitchen. He reached into the refrigerator for a pitcher of filtered water, poured himself a glass and downed the entire contents in a few gulps.

"My panties are hanging in the bathroom to dry. I washed them out last night."

Ethan was pouring another glassful of water, but stopped abruptly and closed his gray-green eyes. When he opened them again his gaze held only blank iciness. "I'll be gone all afternoon. Can you find a store around here to shop for clothes?"

Ethan lived in a fairly upscale neighborhood northwest of Nellis Air Force Base in a newly built, Mediterranean-style condo with an attached garage and—according to the sign at the manager's office—a pool and spa on the premises. It was a world away from her one-room apartment above the shop on the wrong side of the Strip.

"Oh, yes. I'll find my way around. What would you like for dinner tonight? Have you ever tried the Raw diet? I have a wonderful recipe for beets. Or I could make—"

"No dinner. I'll get something on the way home."

"But I want to thank you for letting me stay here."

He rounded the kitchen counter and headed down the hall. "No need."

"But you have to eat. Unless you have plans." Lily followed him, admiring the flex of his thick quads as he walked. "I didn't think about that. Maybe you have plans. What about tomorrow?"

With a sigh, he stopped just inside the bathroom, turned and gripped the door handle. "No plans. I usually just pick something up on the way home. And tomorrow I work." He looked pointedly out into the hallway, then back at her.

"But tomorrow's Sunday. You work all weekend?"

His jaw muscle ticked as he stared at her. "Sometimes."

"Oh. Well, maybe Monday."

His brows lowered and bunched together. "You didn't call your insurance agent last night. Are you going to speak with them today?"

"Um…about that."

He took a step toward her and leaned in. "You *do* have insurance on your place, right?"

Lily breathed in his musky scent and an ache of a different kind spread through her body. "Oh, yes. I do, but…" He should have been intimidating, he was such a big guy, towering over her. A few inches over six feet. A large frame. His jaw was dark with stubble, so utterly masculine.

"But?"

She blinked and tried to remember what they'd been talking about. Oh, yes. Insurance. *Oh, Ethan. There's so much more to life. And I can't wait to show you.* She smiled and waved a hand. "Nothing. I can look it up." She took a step backward, out into the hallway. "Have a nice shower."

He studied her with narrowed eyes and then shut the door. A split second later it jerked open and he tossed her thong out.

Through the door she heard the shower door open and the water turn on. She pictured him tugging the T-shirt over his head and stripping out of his shorts, and had to press a hand to her stomach. A strident feline yowl was followed by a low male grunt, and a moment later the door opened just a crack and Rhett was pitched out. The orange tabby landed easily on his feet and stalked away.

Lily chuckled. *Poor Ethan.*

While he showered, she let Humphrey in, then pulled the towel off Bette's cage and filled her water dispenser. "Good morning, Bette," she greeted her cockatoo.

"Life is like a box of chocolates," the bird squawked.

Lily smiled. "It sure is, sweetie."

As she went back to the bedroom to look for Scarlett, the bathroom door swung open and Ethan strode out with only a towel wrapped around his waist. It reminded her of last night, except this time he didn't even have the boxer briefs underneath. His jaw was clean-shaven now and she caught a whiff of some woodsy aftershave.

He stopped short when he saw her, and cleared his throat. "My clothes." He gestured at the walk-in closet on the opposite wall.

"Of course." She spied Scarlett with her twitchy nose beside the dresser, scooped her up and headed for the hallway.

Lily cuddled the quivering guinea pig under her chin for a few minutes, then busied herself finding the coffee, filters and mugs, and got a pot going. Within ten minutes Ethan emerged from the bedroom dressed in a sharply pressed uniform complete with an air force tie pin and shiny black shoes.

As he stood before the door adjusting his tie Bette squawked. "Fasten your seat belts."

He looked over at the bird and scowled. "It talks?"

"*She* talks. Sometimes. That's Bette. And she must like you because she doesn't talk to just anyone. She was telling you to stay safe today."

Ethan blinked at Lily, his dark look seeming permanent. "I'd appreciate it if you'd keep your menagerie confined to the bedroom at night," he said, glancing away. "The black cat tried to sleep on me and the rodent scratched around on the floor all night."

Lily moved into his line of vision. "Scarlett is not a rodent, she's a guinea pig. And Ingrid likes you, too. That's a good sign."

"Just keep the cats away from the leather, and get something to confine the rodent."

"Don't you like animals, Ethan?" Lily stroked Ingrid's soft black fur.

"Not particularly."

"Well, no wonder your aura is so dark. Do you have anybody you really love?"

He looked blank. "Love?"

"You know." Lily moved closer, tilting her head back to look up at him. "People you care about. Who care about you? Who would be there no matter what? Who love you, warts and all?"

Still no response.

"You know. Like a mom. A mom loves you no matter what. You love your mom, right?"

In a heartbeat his expression turned icy and he glanced at his watch again. "I have to go. Your clothes are in the dryer. There's a spare key in the third cabinet on the right. Lock the door when you leave."

Before she could say anything more, he was out the door.

Lily stared after him, still caressing Ingrid. *Wow.* He wouldn't even talk about his mom. This might be her worst case yet.

Before she left, Lily wandered about the condo, getting a feel for what would help Ethan the most. *Sad. Lonely. Cold.* She shivered and rubbed her arms. It seemed desperate measures might be in order.

PAIN SHOT THROUGH ETHAN'S neck and back every time he moved. It had been a long day. Like the city it was located near, Nellis Air Force Base was never quiet. After briefing his students on their training sortie, he'd taken them out to the test range, flown four runs and then debriefed back at the office.

Now, after hours of sitting hunched over at his desk, filling out reports, he found himself wishing for Lily's talented fingers to massage away the kink in his neck. He could imagine her standing behind him kneading the tense muscles of his neck and shoulders, murmuring soothing words in her soft, oh so feminine voice.

Naked.

He swallowed as the memory of how she'd looked this morning invaded his mind. Bent over to reveal she shaved…everywhere. Her white breasts tipped with pale pink nipples. And he'd caught a glimpse of a tiny jewel in her belly button….

Ethan groaned and shifted in his chair. Even the brief glimpse he'd gotten had burned the image in his brain forever.

Then he remembered she was the reason he hurt.

A bruise the size of an ostrich egg had formed between his shoulder blades where the beam had hit, and trying to sleep on that futon had given him a crick in his neck. Thankfully, he would only have to stay there a couple more nights. Maybe she'd already found another place that would allow pets. He would offer to pay her rent for a month or two until she received her check from the insurance company.

He couldn't have her staying with him indefinitely. But he was honor-bound to help her out, at least temporarily. He *had* been the cause of her losing not only her living quarters, but her livelihood, as well.

Guilt wrenched him. In twenty years with the air force, during countless tours of combat duty, he'd done his share of blowing up structures. But those missions had had a purpose. Destroy enemy outposts. Secure an area. Ensure safety for the ground troops. But not this.

All because he'd lost control of his reactions.

"There you are."

Ethan recognized the voice and winced. Captain Mitch McCabe lounged against the door frame, still wearing his flight suit from this morning's training session.

"Thought the massage was supposed to help with that kind of thing," McCabe said as he pushed off the jamb and sauntered in.

Ethan realized he was rubbing the back of his neck, and snatched up some papers from his desk. "Need something?"

"Yes, sir." McCabe saluted. "I need a SIT REP, sir."

"A situation report?" Ethan couldn't think of anything new to report. Well, nothing McCabe needed to know about.

"About last night, sir. Since Jackson won the wager, he asked for a… Well, how'd it go, sir?"

McCabe's barely contained smirk grated on Ethan's nerves. "It went." He directed his attention back to the papers and shuffled them around.

But instead of leaving, McCabe planted his scrawny butt on the desk and folded his arms across his chest.

"I heard that things—" he cleared his throat "—heated up fast."

Ethan's gaze shot up to the captain, and pain pierced his neck again. "Where'd you hear that?"

He shrugged. "Jackson heard about it on his police scanner. What the hell happened in there?"

Ethan bit back a curse. This crazy situation… "That place broke so many fire codes it was only a matter of time. But the lady will be out of my place by Monday."

"Whoa, you got that delicious strawberry to go home with you? I prefer to stay at a woman's place myself, but whatever works for you, man."

Ethan shot up from his chair. "I am *not* sleeping with that whack job."

The captain was chuckling and shaking his head before Ethan had even finished his sentence. Too late, he realized McCabe had been baiting him. And it had worked.

Ethan had to take control. Regaining his seat along with his temper, he went back to studying the papers in front of him. "We're done here, McCabe. Have a nice weekend."

"You want to shoot some pool tonight? When Jackson's not on cop patrol he's all wrapped up in Keno girl. And Hughes has been a pain in the ass ever since she got back from Langley."

Ethan sometimes stopped by the officers' club on a Saturday night for a game or two with his buddies. But he probably shouldn't leave the kooky lady alone in his condo for any longer than necessary. "No. I'm heading home."

"Hey, it's cool." McCabe nodded and winked. "I understand."

Ethan didn't take the bait this time. He stared his friend down until the man known at Nellis as "Casanova McCabe" finally saluted and headed down the hall.

After sending an email to his commanding officer that he'd be late Monday morning, Ethan headed for home. He'd stopped by the bank this morning, but he still needed to replace his driver's license.

Within fifteen minutes he pulled his SUV into the garage. He opened the door to his condo and stared around the room as he slowly stepped inside. A leafy tree as tall as the ceiling sat in a clay pot beside his television. The sofa was covered in bright yellow, orange and green pillows. And a neon pink beanbag chair sat in the center of the room.

What had she done? Irritation burned through his insides like acid. His stomach growled at the aroma of barbecue wafting from the kitchen. He looked to his left to find the culprit of this reverse home invasion.

Lily was pulling something out of the oven, head banging to the beat of a song only she could hear on her iPod earbuds. Her hair was parted on either side of her head and tied with ribbons beneath her ears, and she wore a baggy pink shirt and a pair of plaid men's shorts that looked as if she'd stolen them off a retiree at a golf course.

She glanced up and saw him, and her eyes widened. "Ethan." She flashed a dazzling smile. "You're home."

Her million-watt grin hit him like blowback from an F-16. Something caught in his throat and he had to clear it. No one called him Ethan. And no one had ever been glad he was home.

Before he could fully push down the unwanted feelings, she was chattering again. "You're just in time for dinner. I made tofu burgers, with sweet potato wedges to help balance your chi. Do you like honeydew?"

"Lily."

"And I want you to try this wine. It's made from mangos, but you're going to love it. Mist says it balances his energies."

"Lily."

Squawk. "You can't handle the truth," the bird called out, clear as a human.

"Rhett, get off." She shoved the orange tabby— Ethan's archenemy—off the closest kitchen bar stool. "Here, Ethan. Sit down and I'll make you a pla—"

"Lily!" He couldn't remember the last time he'd raised his voice.

"Yes, Ethan?"

"Turn off your music."

She reached up, pulled out her earbuds and waited for him expectantly.

"Where did all this stuff come from?" He gestured back into his living room.

"I know. It looks so much better, right?" She grinned.

"You can't just come in here and redecorate."

"Oh, it cost me hardly anything." Her eyes twinkled. "I got all this from the Goodwill store. They have some wonderful stuff. Come on, let's eat." She was on her way back to the kitchen, when Ethan took a step to grab her arm, but he didn't see the rodent in his path and tripped over it. The animal squealed as if it was being tortured. "I thought I told you to get a cage for that thing."

Lily scooped up the long-haired rat. "Oh, poor baby. Are you all right?" Her brows crinkled as they had yesterday. "You're mad about the pillows and stuff. I should have asked first. But I wanted to surprise you." Those big blue eyes gazed up at him. "I'm so sorry I upset you."

He'd expected an argument. Recrimination or tears. But staring into her apologetic eyes, he was appalled at his show of temper. The fury drained from his body like water through a sieve as guilt hit him full force. The poor woman had just lost everything she owned. This was the second time he'd lost command of himself. Around her. "I'm not upset." He unclenched his fists.

"I just couldn't stay here the way it was. The negative energy was bringing me down."

Huh? What was he supposed to say to that? She had a way of confusing him and turning him on at the same time. Not good. He needed to get this conversation back to sounding rational.

Gritting his teeth, he glanced into his living room. It was only a plant and a few pillows. And a kitty litter box he noticed by the back door. And the noisy bird. But it was just for tonight and tomorrow. He could stand it for one day. Then he'd pack it all off with her when she left on Monday. "Fine, it can stay. But the roden—the guinea pig needs to be contained for his own safety."

"Her."

"What?"

"Scarlett. She's a girl."

"Well, she needs a cage."

"But she needs her freedom. No animal should be confined against their—"

"Lily."

"Yes, Ethan?"

He folded his arms across his chest. "It's not negotiable."

She sighed and cuddled the guinea pig under her chin. Then she looked up at him with that beautiful smile. "Well, I suppose every relationship requires compromise. But I want to get one that has a house, and a wheel, and—"

"That's fine. Let's go." He fished his keys from his pocket and headed out the door while Lily set the tray of tofu burgers in the fridge.

Wait a minute. He stopped on the first step. Had she just used the word *relationship?*

3

ETHAN GRABBED A bright red Pet World cart as Lily bounced down the aisle. Sometimes he wondered if she'd been dropped on her head as a child. On the other hand, he also couldn't stop picturing her naked. What kind of sicko did that make him?

"Good evening, sir, can I help you find something?" A teenager with a severe case of acne, dressed in khaki pants and a red polo shirt, stood near the cash registers.

"Guinea pig cages?" Ethan kept an eye on Lily as she rounded a corner into a side aisle.

"Yes, sir, the small pets section is in the back, to the left," the teen answered, as another customer walked up to ask him something.

Of course it would be all the way at the back. Shopping of any kind was a necessary evil. But a pet store? With grim determination Ethan headed deeper into hostile territory, stopping at the corner where he'd last seen Lily.

"Aren't these cute?" She held up several brown stuffed animals. "Rhett would love these. Which one? A catnip hedgehog or a catnip squirrel?"

Yeah. Just what he wanted. To buy the scary feline a toy. "Small pets stuff is farther down the aisle." Ethan moved on, expecting her to follow. And she did, until they passed the intersection.

She squealed. "Oooh, Ethan. These are so adorable."

Maybe if he just kept going she'd put down whatever she'd seen, and get on board with their plan of action.

"It's a Cuddle Pal for Humphrey to lie on. Ethan, you're not looking."

Why couldn't she act like a normal adult? He had better things to do than stand around looking at pet toys with a weird, infuriating female. He rounded on her. "Lily, our goal is to acquire a guinea pig cage. We get in, complete our mission and get out."

She stared at him as if he was the crazy one, then shook her head and laughed.

"What?" He tightened his grip on the handle of the cart.

"This isn't a combat zone. We don't have to save the tropical fish section from reptile terrorist attacks."

He narrowed his eyes. "It's simply a matter of expediency. If you pick up and comment on everything we pass, we'll be here until they close."

"And what would be so bad about that? What else have you got to do tonight?"

"I—" He'd think of something in a second. Surely

there was something he needed to do at home. "That's not the point. The point is there is no reason to examine every single item when you don't intend to buy them."

"The *point*—" she emphasized the word "—is to have fun."

"Fun?"

"You know. That thing you did as a kid? Playing? Cops and robbers? Cowboys and Indians?" She lowered her voice and wiggled her brows. "Doctor and nurse? Didn't you and your friends play?"

"No." *Playing is for sissies.* His dad's words echoed in his head.

Her smile disappeared. "Oh."

Avoiding the pity in her eyes, he pushed the cart toward the back of the store.

She caught up to him and tucked her arm in his. "Where did you grow up?"

"You're the psychic, you tell me."

"Actually, that's my friend, Sunny. She's amazing. But I like guessing games. How about after three wrong guesses you tell me the right answer?"

Ethan sighed. Nothing was going to stop this woman. "Fine."

"Okay. Ooh, this is fun. Hmm…" She put her finger to her lips and tapped. "Let's see, um, Detroit, Michigan."

"Nope."

"Is it south, east or west of Michigan?"

"That wasn't part of the deal." He bit back a smile.

"Humph." She pouted. And it looked sexy, damn it.

She wasn't going to ge—

"South Dakota."

He came to a halt and turned to face her. "How did you do that?"

She wiggled her eyebrows. "You twitched when I said the word *south*. And you don't have a Southern drawl, so I knew it wasn't South Carolina."

He…twitched? "Huh," he grunted, the only way he could convey a grudging respect for her. No one had ever read him like that.

"Omigosh, that was fun. Okay, what city? Gosh, I don't know very many cities in South Dakota. I know about Mount Rushmore, and the Black Hills, and Crazy Horse."

"You've never heard of it." He barely remembered it. He remembered shoveling snow, taking out the trash, homework. But not playing with friends. His only memories before that were of sitting around in the hospital waiting room.

Lily shrugged one shoulder. "I still want to know. Is it Sioux Falls?"

He sighed. If he didn't answer, he figured she'd bug him until he did. "Belle Fourche. It's in the northwest part of the state," he continued, as she opened her mouth. "Just north of the Black Hills National Forest."

"*Belle* means *beautiful* in French. I bet it's beautiful country up there."

"I guess." He'd been too desperate to get away to care. He'd joined the air force right out of high school, and could count on one hand the number of times he'd been home since.

"Are your parents still there?"

They weren't the snowbird type. It would take an act of God to pry them out of their house. His mom with her blank stare spent her life in the kitchen, cooking and cleaning, and his father sat coldly at the table with his paper.

"I'm sorry." Lily squeezed his arm. "Have they… passed on?"

He resumed his mission in the small pets section. "They're fine." As far as he knew. Last time he'd received a letter from his mother was seven months ago. Right after Christmas. After he'd sent his usual card with a check.

"Any brothers or sisters?"

Ethan gritted his teeth as a familiar pang hit his chest. "What is it with you? What do you care?"

Lily stopped in her tracks and pulled her hand away. "Oh, Ethan. Your aura just now. I'm sorry I brought up something so painful."

Denying the pain was on the tip of his tongue. But for some reason he couldn't. Without a word, he continued down the main aisle.

Lily caught up to him and again slipped her arm through his. "So, what do you do in the air force?"

He raised a brow.

"Oh, right. Three guesses. Okay, fighter pilot."

He shrugged. "Was. I'm an air combat instructor now."

"Air combat? As in teaching maneuvers? Like the Red Baron?"

"Lily." Thankfully, they'd reached the back of the store. He turned left. "We don't have to do the whole get-to-know-each-other thing."

"Eeethan." She said his name as if he'd just burped the alphabet at the queen's tea. "Of course we do. But I'll tell you about me for a little while."

He almost stopped her. But she was going to chatter about something, so he might as well… Okay, so he was curious.

"I grew up all over the West Coast. San Fran, L.A., San Diego. And everywhere in between. It was usually just my mom and me. But sometimes we lived with my mom's boyfriends."

Lily gasped and disappeared down an aisle to the right. "Omigawd, Ethan. They have Halloween costumes for pets."

Wait a minute. What about her mom's boyfriends? Why had she said the word *boyfriend* as if it was cow dung? Had any of them hurt her? Ethan pulled to a stop when he spied her on a side aisle holding up a devil costume and a bear in a red T-shirt.

"Wouldn't Humphrey look adorable as Winnie the Pooh?"

She was insane. That was the only explanation. "You didn't finish."

"Finish?" She put the costumes back and returned to his side.

"About your mother's boyfriends."

"Not much to tell." Lily changed directions again to stroll down the main aisle, and he followed. "I never knew my dad. My mom was really young when she found out she was pregnant with me, and she said he freaked."

Ethan wondered which was worse—his father or no father?

"I think his family sent her some money, and she went to college. It was just me and her for a while until… she fell in love with this guy and seemed to just go crazy. She quit a good job, moved to be with him, and then it didn't work out. She was crushed." Lily stopped and looked at Ethan. "But you know what's crazy? A few years later, she did it again."

"So, that's why you moved around a lot?"

Lily shrugged. "I didn't mind. Every new city was an adventure. A chance to see what fate had in store for me in each new place."

Karma. Fate. Who lived their life like that? "So, did karma tell you to buy an herb shop in Vegas?"

Her smile faltered and she hitched her purse higher on her shoulder. "I came out here with my best friend right after high school. He wanted to be a croupier and I…" She gave a one-shouldered shrug. "I went to massage school."

Ethan scowled, certain there was more she wasn't telling him. But they'd finally located the small pet cages. Then there was bedding. And that house he'd agreed to. And Lily loaded one of those hollow plastic balls an animal could roll around in into the cart, as well.

"Can we go now?" he asked.

"You really hate shopping, don't you?"

"Doesn't everyone?"

She shook her head. "Theo didn't. He loved shopping with me."

"Theo was your friend?"

She bit her lip and Ethan wanted to soothe it with his thumb. "And my husband."

Husband? She was married?

"He was killed in Iraq five years ago."

Killed. Guilt oozed past the wall of Ethan's perfectly legitimate detachment. She'd been so young to be widowed. "I'm sorry." He looked into her eyes and then couldn't look away. All he could think about was that horrible cliché about drowning in pools of…something. But that's what it felt like. They were exactly the turquoise color of the Caribbean.

Thankfully, she broke eye contact and said, "It's okay."

Without thinking, he tucked his knuckle under her chin and lifted her face. "I've lost friends in battle, too. It's never okay."

Her eyes filled with tears, and before he could stop her, she stepped close and wrapped her arms around his waist. "No one's ever said that before. But it's true, isn't it?"

Just as he was regretting the rare moment of spontaneity, she sniffed and stepped back. "Thank you." She pulled her shirt up and wiped the tears off her cheeks, and then gave him a brilliant smile. "Well, so much for helping you have fun tonight."

Stunned, he stared at her, his arms still held away from his body. He'd liked having her cheek against his chest. He'd liked the feel of her body pressed to his.

She took a deep breath. "Okay. Let's go home now."

Relieved, he pointed their cart full of goodies toward the front before she changed her mind.

AFTER REHEATING AND offering him the tofu burgers, which he declined, Lily began setting up the cage for the guinea pig.

Ethan retreated to his weight room and worked out an extra fifteen minutes, then went a couple rounds with his punching bag for good measure. After a quick shower, he slipped on jeans and a T-shirt and braved the main room.

She was messing with the rodent when he entered the kitchen. "Good night."

"You're going to bed?" She abandoned the cage and stood.

Ethan tried to look away, but his gaze wouldn't obey his survival instincts. She'd changed into a pair of over-size men's boxers and a tight tank top. And she must have showered earlier while he was working out, because her hair was damp. It was swept up off her neck, all her strawberry curls held with a clip. She smelled like some kind of sweet flower.

He glanced at his watch. "It's ten o'clock."

"And you always go to bed at ten?"

Always. He shrugged. "Usually."

"But you haven't eaten anything."

"I'm not hungry."

"Would you like that glass of wine? It's—"

"I don't drink."

She blinked. "Ever?"

"No."

"Are you…a recovering alcoholic?"

He frowned. "No."

"You have some religious strictures against alcoholic beverages?"

Where was this going? "No."

"Oh." She cocked her head, studying him.

There was an awkward silence, and all Ethan could think about was how she'd looked this morning.

"Well…" He gave her a curt nod. "Good n—"

"Wait." She rushed to the refrigerator, opened it and bent over to pull out one of his dinner plates. "I almost forgot. I made this for you." On the plate was a crusty golden cake with whipped cream and strawberries on top.

Ethan's stomach growled and his mouth watered. "Is that—"

"Strawberry shortcake." She confirmed his suspicion with a grin. His all-time-favorite dessert. How had she known?

Setting it on the counter, she turned to grab a smaller plate from the cabinet and his largest chopping knife from the block. "Please say you'll eat just a bite."

Ethan told himself he didn't want to hurt her feelings. And he *was* weak from hunger. He reached over the counter, swiped a fork from a drawer and dropped onto one of the bar stools.

Before he knew it he'd finished off two huge slices and was licking the fork. Suddenly, he realized Lily was sitting beside him, sucking on a strawberry, watching him with half-closed eyes.

Swirling her tongue around the red fruit, she wrapped her lips around the fat end. Then she closed her eyes and moaned as she bit into it and chewed.

That was the oldest trick in the book. But there was a reason women still used it. Because it worked.

He stared at her, fighting the pull, fighting the need.

Her tongue swept a trickle of juice from her lips, and Ethan groaned. A man could take only so much temptation. He grasped her shoulders and pulled her against him, watching her mouth part in surprise right before he took possession of it.

She opened up to him as if she'd been waiting all her life for him to kiss her, wrapping her arms around his neck and rubbing her stiff nipples against his chest.

That trampled the last vestiges of his control. He slid an arm around her back and crushed her to him, devouring her mouth, bruising her lips. She whimpered, which only served to ratchet up his lust. His cock surged and pulsed. It'd been too long since he'd been with a woman, and his body was making up for lost time. His free hand cupped her breast and squeezed, his thumb rubbing across the puckered peak. She was a perfect fit, filling his palm. So soft, yet firm. He wanted a taste.

He stood, lifting her with him, and carried her to the couch. Shoving pillows out of the way, he laid her down, dropping on top of her. His lips moved over hers and his tongue swept in to taste her whipped cream and strawberries. But he wanted more. He had to taste her breasts, and lick the pink nipples that he'd seen in his mind all day long.

"Wait, Ethan," she murmured as he kissed his way down her neck, lifting her tank top to expose the soft globes. She tried to pull away, but he held fast, denying her release. His body was in command, his cock straining for completion of the act. Needing to touch her flesh, he brought his mouth to one tight peak and suckled.

"Hold on." She wriggled beneath him. "Hold on!" She brought her palms to either side of his face and tried to push him off, but he only growled and moved to nip at her other breast while his hands slipped beneath her boxers, cupped her butt and pressed her against his hard, aching erection.

"Ethan," she gasped, fear in her voice.

The haze of lust cleared. He froze, shocked, and lifted himself off her. He was shaking. What was he doing, forcing himself on a woman? Had he lost his mind?

No. He'd lost the ability to reason. And that was why he never allowed himself to be this much out of control.

He shoved himself off the couch, tripping over the damned beanbag chair. He couldn't stay here right now. He had to leave. Grabbing his key, he headed for the door.

"Wait, Ethan. Don't go."

He had to. He couldn't even look at her. He wasn't sure he could ever face her again. He'd probably scared her to death. And yet mixed in somewhere with his guilt and disgust was anger. At her. For making him lose control.

Because what was worse, he'd scared himself.

4

ETHAN GRADY WAS PROVING to be more of a challenge than Lily had ever dealt with.

After he rushed out, she stared at the door, her whole body trembling. She touched her fingers to her lips. They were swollen and still tingled. She'd never been kissed so thoroughly, as if she were the only woman he'd ever wanted, and he would have her and damn the consequences. And her breasts where he'd caressed her... She gently covered her still-hard nipple, so sensitive after Ethan's contact. She'd known there was a powerful passion inside him, strictly contained. And Goddess, she'd unleashed it tonight. His sacral chakra had surely been unblocked.

Wasn't that what she'd wanted? Hadn't that been her purpose in feeding him the strawberries? But the intensity of his passion had overwhelmed her.

This wasn't like when she'd helped Ben last year. She'd taken one look at his sluggish, muddy-brown aura in the veterinarian's office and known she could help him. At first it'd been as simple as changing his diet and introducing him to meditation. Then she'd encouraged Ben to channel his negative energy into positive acts. After a couple of months he'd finally gotten the courage to call his ex and speak to his kids for the first time in years.

With Ben things had been strictly platonic. He'd still been in love with his ex, and had only needed a friend.

But Ethan was…different.

Lily washed the dishes and straightened the kitchen, filled up everyone's food and water, and swept the floors, all the while contemplating what she should do next.

This was just a small setback. The man needed to get laid, that was for sure. And so did she, obviously. She hadn't had sex in months and her chi was feeling out of balance. And it made sense that unblocking his sexual energies so quickly after so many years of obstruction would cause an inability to handle the sexual surge. She should have been prepared for that.

Especially after his revelations in the pet store. He'd never played as a child? And something about siblings upset him. He'd already refused to talk about his mother. It didn't take a psychic to sense something momentous had happened in his childhood to block his heart chakra. Would he ever trust her enough to tell her what had happened? Lily wondered.

She shouldn't have discouraged him tonight. What if she'd done more harm than good? Maybe she was wrong for him. Or maybe she'd interpreted the tarot wrongly? What should she do now?

She needed guidance.

Throwing on her tennis shoes, she took The Pumpkin to Sunny's. Despite the late hour—it was after midnight—Sunny answered the door to her psychic shop before Lily even raised her hand to knock.

"Show-off," Lily teased as she hugged the older lady and stepped inside.

"I've missed you, hon." The silver-haired psychic bussed Lily's cheek with a kiss and waved her inside. "I hope you're making progress with your young man. It's distressing to see the charred remains of your shop every time I look out my window." She shook her head as she waddled through her store and sat at her divining table.

Lily stopped to study the burned building across the street. She expected to feel sorrow, distress. Instead, a profound sense of peace washed through her. In her mind she saw the shop rebuilt, and felt a sense of new beginnings. She smiled and joined Sunny at the table. Maybe this was what she'd come here for. But one question still remained.

"Sunny, I'm afraid I messed up. Maybe I was mistaken about the lieutenant colonel. Maybe—"

"The tarot showed the Tower card, honey. Destructive forces at work. And who caused the fire that brought about the destruction?"

"I know, but Ethan, he's so… He's more repressed than anybody I've ever helped before. He's so intense."

"And his intensity frightens you?"

Lily started to deny it, but stopped herself. She *had* been afraid. Sex for her had always been pleasant, fun, relaxing. But her response to Ethan's kisses had been visceral…potent. She'd sought to gentle his fervor, to show him how to slow down and enjoy the moment. But there'd been something in his eyes when he'd growled at her. Something feral. She hadn't feared for her safety. But she'd wanted to pull back because she'd been afraid of such a powerful sexual encounter.

"I think…" she scrutinized Sunny's knowing gaze "…when we kissed, the power that surged between us felt dangerous."

Sunny's questioning eyes flared, and she cocked her head. "You must ask yourself why."

Lily drew in a deep breath. "I think he's not used to letting himself feel emotion. And all those closed-off feelings came pouring out and overcame him. That's why he left tonight. I'm not sure how to change that for him. Getting him accustomed to dealing with his emotions could take weeks, maybe months. And I'm not sure how long he'll let me stay."

The psychic nodded and her bangles and bracelets clinked as she reached for her tarot cards and handed them to Lily. "Formulate the question in your mind as you shuffle."

Lily cleared her thoughts and then concentrated on Ethan's face. *How am I meant to help Lieutenant Colonel Ethan Grady?* She shuffled the cards three times, then handed them back.

Sunny laid them out in the Celtic Cross pattern, then turned the middle one over. "The Fool. A young traveler willing to leap into the unknown and start anew."

This card represented the questioner. Lily.

Sunny turned the next one over and smiled. "The King of Swords. A skilled warrior. Highly analytical. That is your young man, yes?"

Lily bit her lip and nodded.

"It's the same as before," Sunny continued. "He crosses your path. He is your future."

"My immediate future," Lily corrected.

The older woman shrugged and turned over the third card: the questioner's goal or destiny. "Death. The questioner must accept change so that rebirth can occur."

"Could that mean the fire?"

The psychic shook her head. "No. This is more personal. Maybe...an emotional death and rebirth."

Lily frowned. How could her changing her own emotions help Ethan? More likely she was meant to change his.

Sunny turned over the rest of the cards in the cross one at a time. The fourth card, representing a distant past that affects the present, was the Queen of Swords, reversed. A dangerous enemy with a closed mind.

"Maybe someone in Ethan's past was closed off from him?" Lily guessed. "That's where he learned to keep his emotions in check."

"Perhaps," Sunny replied. She turned over the fifth card. "The Nine of Rods. The situation will worsen before it gets better."

Lily nodded, accepting this as truth. Look what had happened tonight. But that also told her it *would* get better.

As the rest were revealed Lily opened her mind to the universe to interpret their meaning.

When the Queen of Cups was turned over, a flash of certainty hit her gut. The queen drank deeply from the cup of life. This was the sign that Lily should continue showing Ethan that life was meant to be full of joy, not sadness. But how?

The last card was the King of Wands. This card had never come up for her before. She looked at Sunny.

"The King of Wands concentrates on goals. Collaboration in professional projects brings great rewards."

Professional projects? What project could she and Ethan collaborate on? Lily had no idea, but her instinct told her this was important. Ethan was a very goal-oriented man. They just needed to find a common goal.

Sunny studied her. "Does this help at all?"

"I don't know," she answered, still thinking. Then she shrugged. "But I'll keep it in mind." Her first order of business was to get Ethan back on the horse, so to speak. They had some unfinished sex to have.

Sunny's light blue eyes sparkled with approval. "Everything's going to work out with you and your young man." She smiled and wiggled her brows. "Ahh, enjoy the journey, child."

IF IT WASN'T ALMOST midnight, and if he hadn't left the house without shoes, Ethan would be jogging on the trail around the park by his house. A good run would burn off all the tension tonight had brought.

But rational people didn't go jogging this late at night, and certainly not in their bare feet.

So he'd gone to his office. The lieutenant at the security gate had waved Ethan through without a second glance at his ID. Ethan showed up at the air base defense school to teach night maneuvers with enough regularity that nobody questioned his presence at this late hour.

Once on base, he felt a sense of normalcy returned. The smell of jet fuel and burning rubber on concrete. The sound of mechanics' tools clinking in the hangar, and jet engines powering up or revving down. All was familiar and routine. In his office, neat and tidy, paperwork awaited that he knew how to deal with. Here, at least, his world was logical. He knew what to expect. Chaos wasn't allowed.

Even as he was leaning back in his chair, appreciating peace and order, a loud crash from along the corridor disrupted the quiet. Ethan jumped, unlocked the bottom drawer and pulled out his semiautomatic. Within a few seconds he was down the hall. Another sound, like scuffling, came from McCabe's office. Probably had a lady friend in there.

But there was no moaning. No gasping. No rhythmic pounding. A shadow moved past the obscured glass panel in the door. Ethan turned the knob and burst in, gun aimed.

"Geez, Grady." Captain Alexandria Hughes, with a hand on her chest, was standing on a chair, reaching up to the top of the bookshelf behind McCabe's desk. "You scared the crap out of me." She let out a swift breath and motioned for him to close the door.

"Likewise," Ethan replied as he lowered his gun and shut the door behind him. She was wearing her usual weekend uniform—an old pair of Wranglers and a faded KISS T-shirt. "What's the prank this time?"

She opened her mouth to answer, but he put a hand up to stop her. "Never mind. I don't want to know."

She grinned. "Probably best."

"Aren't you two getting a little old for these games?"

"Hey!" Hughes pierced him with a glare. "*He* started it."

Ethan coughed. "That was twelve years ago. You were both cadets at the Air Force Academy."

She just shrugged. "After what he did to me last month? You know how many men showed up at my house thinking I'd made dates with them from that matchmaking website? McCabe's gonna pay for that."

"And what about all those women you sent here back in May while he was celibate?"

Her eyes sparked with mischief and her grin widened. "He deserved that. After the way he treats women."

"So, you've become his conscience now?"

"Well, somebody ought to. It's not like he's got one of his own."

Ethan folded his arms over his chest. "You can't change who he is, Hughes. Some guys just aren't meant to settle down and have a family." Himself included. He was almost forty. He wouldn't know what to do with a wife and kid. Of course, he wasn't like McCabe, either. Bedding everyone in a skirt within a hundred-mile radius.

But Ethan clearly needed to satisfy his physical needs more regularly if his behavior tonight was any indication. Jumping on a woman with as much finesse as a high school kid and scaring her to death was about as low as a man could go in his book. As soon as Lily moved out this week, he'd make more of an effort to find a compatible sexual partner.

"He used to want a family more than anything." Hughes's grin had faded. Ethan recalled they'd been talking about McCabe.

"Remember that movie about the divorced woman whose friends tell her she's at a crossroads in her life, and send her to Italy?" Hughes put her hands on her hips and met his gaze without a shade of guilt. "Well, McCabe took a wrong turn at that crossroads and he's been on a path to hell ever since."

This conversation had gotten way too touchy-feely. "Since when do you go see chick flicks?" A tough gal from a ranch in the Texas Panhandle, Captain Alex Hughes usually shunned all things feminine, ripping a new one out of anyone who dared treat her like a woman.

She cocked an eyebrow. "There are a lot of things you don't know about me."

Ethan frowned. "I know there are other things you

could be doing on a Saturday night." Clearly, Hughes needed to find a compatible partner, also.

"Are you saying I have no life?" She glared at him. "'Cause I totally do. I could be dating a Navy SEAL right now. He…" A look of panic filled her eyes. "He wasn't a bad guy for a squid," she finished lamely.

"Okay. Well. Carry on, Captain." Ethan turned and reached for the doorknob.

"Wait a minute." With lightning speed, Hughes hopped off the chair and blocked his way. "What are *you* doing awake after ten o'clock at night?"

No way was he going to explain the events of the past twenty-four hours to anyone. At best, he'd be listening to arson jokes the rest of his career. "Forgot some paperwork."

She looked down and shock registered on her face. "And where are your shoes?" Bending over, she reached out and picked a wad of black cat hair off the bottom of his jeans. "And since when do you have a pet?"

LILY SAT CROSS-LEGGED on the floor of the main room of the condo Sunday evening, trying to meditate. She'd left the lights off, lit a candle and tried to empty her mind of all the ways the rest of the night could go so wrong.

Doubt wiggled together with guilt in her belly. She'd made Ethan feel as if his passion was a bad thing. And now she had to make it up to him. Get back on the horse, so to speak. Tonight.

If he ever came home.

He'd returned in the early hours of the morning,

showered, changed into his uniform and headed out again. Lily had long before that gone to bed, but she'd been aware of his presence.

Finally, she heard the garage door open and his SUV pull in. It was after nine o'clock now. She jumped up and pulled the carob meringue pie she'd made earlier out of the fridge, and set it on the bar.

When he walked through the door, the air changed. It seemed to crackle and spark. Lily's breathing turned ragged just from her staring at him, standing so straight and inflexible in his uniform. His aura was darker than ever, and there were shadows under his eyes.

He stood just inside the door, his expression neutral, but his face showed the strain of the past twenty-four hours. She could sense his internal struggle. He didn't want to be here with her. Yet he was too honorable, too brave to avoid a difficult situation.

"*Squawk.* Make my day," Bette called from her cage.

"*Namaste,* Ethan." Lily's own voice sounded so quavery. Not good. He'd think she was still afraid of him. Perhaps she should have chosen something different to wear. The lightweight sundress had seemed the perfect balance between seductive and cheerful earlier. Now, it seemed too thin to hide the fact that her nipples had tightened to the point of pain.

Ethan cleared his throat. "I wanted to apologize."

"There's no need. You're a passionate man. I've examined my feelings, and realize I was merely frightened of the forceful energy between us."

"I hope I didn't hurt you."

"Oh, no. I was never afraid of that. I was totally into it."

His face creased into confusion mixed with disbelief.

"Have you eaten?"

He glanced past her at the pie, and a gleam of desire passed so quickly in his eyes she almost missed it. "I picked up something earlier at work."

Lily smiled. Her guess about his repressed sweet tooth had been right. Hopefully, she could tempt him again. "Maybe just a piece of pie, then?" She grabbed up the dessert and presented it to him with all the flair of showcasing letters on *Wheel of Fortune.*

His gaze locked on the pie. His Adam's apple bobbed as he swallowed. He licked his lips. *Poor guy.* More internal struggling against indulging his passions.

Setting the pie back on the bar, Lily grabbed a plate and a knife and cut a large slice. As if not quite aware of what he was doing, he moved to the bar and sat on a stool. She'd barely set the plate in front of him before he snatched up a fork and dug in.

After the first bite, he looked younger. The lines on his face eased. His aura lightened to a soft grayish-yellow. Lily cut him another slice and set it on his plate. As he ate he seemed to relax. His eyelids drooped. It was almost ten o'clock. He couldn't have gotten much sleep last night.

She covered up the pie and put it in the fridge.

Cleaned up the dishes. Put the towel over Bette's cage. "Well, good night."

"Hey." He stopped her as she headed down the hall.

She turned back.

"Thanks for the pie."

She smiled. "You're welcome."

After watching him go into the spare room, she left her door slightly ajar, brushed her teeth and then crawled into Ethan's big comfy bed.

And waited.

5

LILY HEARD THE CLANK of weights and the sound of Ethan punching the bag. She listened as the shower turned on, and pictured him naked, water cascading down his body. She waited for the sound of his door closing, and finally, nothing but silence.

Every erogenous zone on her body hummed with anticipation as she climbed out of bed, padded softly to the other bedroom and slowly opened the door.

There was just enough streetlight from the window to make her way around the workout equipment. As she approached the futon she drew her nightshirt over her head and dropped it on the floor.

Ethan lay on his stomach facing away from her, his arms folded beneath his head and one knee bent. His shoulder blades cast shadows across the muscled planes of his bare back to the waistband of his briefs.

With deliberate slowness she lifted the sheet and slid in beside him, trailing a gentle hand along the slope of his spine. She followed with her lips, caressing his skin with her mouth.

A low sound escaped his throat and he stirred, turning onto his back. Lily rose and straddled his hips, feeling his cock, already hard as stone, push against her clit. She ran her palms from his rippled abs up to his pecs, reveling in the firmness and heat of his flesh.

He moaned, but his heavy lids remained closed. "What are you doing?" he mumbled.

"I want you, Ethan. Make love to me." She leaned down, flattened her breasts against his chest and placed a soft kiss on the corner of his mouth. Another kiss along his jaw. And another.

He frowned and finally opened his eyes. "I don't think that's a good idea." His voice was lower, raspy, and his hands were clenched at his sides.

"Okay." She wouldn't force him. It had to be what he wanted, too. She climbed off him and stood, looking for her nightshirt.

"Wait." He sat up, gripped her arm and pulled her back down.

With his gaze locked on hers he cupped the back of her head, then covered her mouth with his. He kissed her leisurely, thoroughly, until she felt her veins were on fire and her bones melting. "I'll try to take it slower this time," he said against her lips.

"There's no need," she reassured him, delving beneath his briefs to encircle his rigid length. He was just as impressive as she'd suspected, longer than her hand

and so thick her thumb and middle finger wrapped around him didn't meet.

Raising his hips to push against her palm, he moaned into her mouth and then broke the kiss. "Careful." He stilled her stroking hand, then yanked off his briefs and tossed them. "I have condoms in my room."

Lily smiled. "I brought them in here this afternoon." Leaning over the futon's side, she snatched one from the pile she'd planted underneath it.

When she looked back at Ethan, holding up the foil square in triumph, his teeth flashed white in the darkness. He was smiling. Her heart did a little flip.

Ripping open the package, she straddled him again and started to roll the condom on, but he stopped her. "Not so fast." He cupped her breasts in his palms and lifted one to his mouth. His tongue swirled around her nipple, teasing, just before his lips latched on and suckled.

With a gasp she clutched the back of his head as an arousing ache shot to her core, pulsing in her empty, yearning passage. He moved to the other nipple, licking and sucking it with equal enthusiasm. Her fingers combed through his short dark hair, holding on as the sensation of her flesh in his mouth sent stinging shards of pleasure through her body. Her skin tingled, her clit throbbed and she rubbed it against his cock. "Ethan," she moaned, begging for more.

His lips dragged down the side of her breast, and he gently coaxed her onto her back while he rose to his knees and placed kisses down to her stomach and farther. Her breathing hitched when he pushed her thighs wide and buried his head between them, mumbling an inarticulate sound of delight.

Even as he held her open and thrust his tongue inside, she could sense his restraint. Gone was last night's desperate wildness, as if he'd locked down that untamed animal within.

Not that she was complaining. She'd never been with a man so determined with his mouth and fingers. Unable to keep from writhing beneath him, she gripped his head and thanked the universe as he took her swollen clit between his lips and set fire to her core. With her ankles locked around his back, she closed her eyes and let her body rock with spasms.

Limp and out of breath, she flung her arms above her head and moaned long and low. "Goddess," she gasped.

Ethan ran a hand over his mouth and jaw as he crawled up to lie beside her. She gave him a lazy smile, but she couldn't read his expression. He played with her nipples while he rustled around in the sheets and found the condom she'd dropped. The stimulus kept her inner passage contracting as he effortlessly rolled on the protection and moved over her.

Finally, he looked into her eyes. Who was this man? This sexy, talented, harsh man who'd just rocked her world? She realized that, until now, she'd only been with boys. Boys who needed her, but weren't particularly concerned about what *she* might need. But Ethan was. He seemed to know exactly what she needed.

Bringing his head down, he nibbled the sensitive spot between her neck and shoulder and pushed inside her.

Lily stiffened as another climax pulsed through her like a current of electricity. He must have felt her inner muscles contract, for he made a low, sensual sound deep in his throat. The sensation of his cock filling her was so good, so right. He belonged in her. With her.

She threw her arms around his neck and buried her nose behind his ear and cried out with each thrust as he moved in her, shorter and harder and faster. His arms tightened around her and Lily felt as one with him and hugged him to her. His breath came in short puffs until he drove into her one last time and shuddered in release.

But before she could soak up the positive energies humming between them, he rolled to his side. His chest heaved with deep, gulping breaths, but Lily knew he'd already distanced himself from her. She wasn't sure his detachment had ever been breached, not even at the end.

As if to prove her right, he got up and headed for the bathroom.

Suddenly cold, she shivered and drew the sheet and blanket over her. She lay there feeling alone and uncertain.

Her emotions still churned in turmoil as Ethan came back and climbed in beside her. He'd washed up—she assumed—and put on a fresh pair of briefs. But instead of taking her in his arms and snuggling, he kept his distance.

The feeling hit her like a punch to the stomach. Her eyes filled with tears she didn't want to shed. Painful, negative energy filled her and surrounded her.

Squeezing her eyes shut, she slid off the futon, grabbed up her nightshirt and stumbled across the hall. A silent sob escaped. How could anyone make love as exquisitely as he had, and remain so unmoved? His sacral chakra was lighter, but the others were still blocked.

She flopped onto the big bed and let go of the negativity. Tonight hadn't been a total failure.

CAPTAIN MITCHELL MCCABE pulled his Jeep into his parking space at Nellis Monday morning fresh from the bed of…well, he couldn't think of her name just now, but they'd had a fun time. Sort of. A little. Okay, so he'd been bored. That happened sometimes, didn't it? Not every woman could leave a guy panting for more.

There'd been nothing wrong with what's-her-name. Tall, blonde, curvy. Just the way he liked them. Except lately every woman he met seemed to have some irritating habit. Either she laughed too much, or she pouted all the time. Or she refused to eat. Or she came on too strong. What was up with women? Why couldn't they be uncomplicated?

Even Hughes. Used to be she was always up-front. No games, no lies, no bullshit. But lately she'd been in a pissy mood and he had no idea what her problem was. Used to be he could count on her after work for a couple of beers and a good game of pool. She was his wingman. But not lately.

And damn it, he missed that.

After stopping by the break room for coffee, Mitch strode to his office, plopped into his desk chair and booted up his PC. He froze with the disposable cup halfway to his mouth.

There was a new icon on his screen, front and center. It was a link to a video. Mitch grinned. He'd been waiting for Hughes to launch her next attack.

Good ol' Hughes. They'd been pulling pranks on each other so long, he'd feel like an amputee if they ever stopped. Even when she'd transferred to Langley they'd somehow managed to get each other long distance.

After hesitating a moment, he clicked on the vid.

The camera had been perfectly placed to get a view of the hallway just outside Hughes's apartment. Hughes stepped out of the elevator with some guy. As they approached the guy slung his arm over her shoulders, and when they stopped in front of her door they faced each other and talked a minute. She nodded and the next moment they were sucking face like there was no tomorrow. Hughes barely got her lock open before they tumbled across the threshold, ripping at each other's clothes. But before she shut the door, she looked directly at the camera, gave it a thumbs-up and winked.

Mitch rubbed his stomach, feeling a bit queasy. Maybe the coffee creamer had expired. But he didn't have time to think about it because the video didn't end there. Over and over, one after another, Hughes brought some strange guy to her apartment, kissed him sense-less and winked at the camera before she shut the door. There must've been a dozen, maybe more. Strangers from that dating service he'd set her up on.

He shoved back from his desk and paced. This wasn't funny. With network admin what it was, anybody could see this.

He stalked down the hall and around the corner and burst into Hughes's office, slamming the door behind him. "Are you trying to ruin your career?"

She didn't budge from her chair. She was leaning back with her feet crossed at the ankle, propped on her desk. Her hands were clasped behind her head and she had an irritating smirk on her face. "How would I do that?"

"Alex, this isn't funny. You have to take that vid down. You have a reputation as a top-notch flight in-structor. This could be seen as behavior unbecoming of an officer. Is this the way you want your fellow officers to see you? Like some slut who sleeps with every guy she—"

Damn.

She chuckled. "Aww, McCabe. I didn't know you cared."

"You didn't sleep with them." Mitch didn't even bother to phrase it as a question. "All those guys. They were all in on it."

Hughes shrugged. "Maybe some."

How many? How many had she slept with for real?

Even though his stomach was still churning, Mitch forced a smile. "Slut."

Hughes full-out grinned. "Manwhore." She dropped her feet and arms, and sat forward. "You were really getting worked up there, McCabe."

Yeah, he had, hadn't he? He forced his clenched fists open and flexed his fingers. He had to hand it to her. Damn, she'd punked him but good. So why wasn't he slapping her on the back and vowing to get even? Why was he desperately trying to think of a way to find out how many of those guys she'd slept with?

A quick knock on the door was the only warning before Lieutenant Colonel Grady stepped in. "Captain Hughes, I need—" He looked up from a stack of papers and saw McCabe. "Don't you have a class this morning?"

Damn. Mitch looked at his TAG Heuer. Air combat maneuvers at 09:30. He glanced at Hughes, who had stood at attention when Grady walked in. She had a weird expression on her face and he realized he hadn't come back with some smart-ass remark. Her expression cleared. The corners of her mouth turned up and she gestured at the door with her chin. *You better go. We'll talk later.* She hadn't said it out loud, but she didn't have to.

He smiled and nodded back at her. *Good one, Hughes.*

CAPTAIN ALEXANDRIA HUGHES, 99th Air Base Squadron, waited until Mitch left before she let out her breath and dropped her smile. *He'd called her Alex.*

"What was that all about?" Grady probed, eyeing her closely.

"What was what, sir?" Alex gave him her most innocent look. Besides, even she wasn't sure what that had been. She'd wanted Mitch to realize how he looked to her. And that part of the plan, she thought, had worked pretty well. The second part? She was honest enough with herself to admit that this prank had ulterior motives. She'd wanted to make him see her as a woman. Not in a romantic type of way. Just…in an "I'm a sexy, desirable female" way. That stupid remark he'd made about her not being a real woman still ticked her off.

Time was she'd done everything in her power to be thought of as just one of the guys.

"This has something to do with your prank, right?" Grady asked.

She shrugged. "Saturday night you said you didn't want to know, sir."

He narrowed his eyes and studied her for several excruciating seconds. If he was hoping to break her, he'd be waiting until the cows came home. And she knew something about cattle. She'd helped her daddy round up herds before she could drive a car.

When she didn't give, Grady heaved a sigh and shook his head.

She took a closer look at the lieutenant colonel. His jaw had spots where he'd missed them with the razor, and there were dark circles under his bloodshot eyes. And his tie was crooked. Grady never appeared less than perfect. If she didn't know better, she'd say he'd been out drinking all night. But the man never indulged.

"Are you all right, sir?"

He scowled and a muscle under his left eye ticked. "Why wouldn't I be? What did McCabe tell you?"

Alex blinked in disbelief. Mitch hadn't told her a thing. But Grady's voice sounded…agitated. Grady was never agitated. What did Mitch know that she didn't? This, coupled with Grady's presence here at midnight Saturday, told her something strange was going on.

"No one's told me anything." She quickly went to rearrange some papers on her desk. "But I'm a good listener if you need an ear. Sir."

She felt rather than saw Grady stiffen. "I have a situation, but I'm handling it. Now about these reports from the test range…"

Grady droned on about the trainees reports and Alex tried to pay attention and nod at the right places, but her mind was racing. Situation? What on earth had happened this weekend?

Mitch knew.

And as soon as she tracked him down for lunch, he was going to tell her.

Until then, she needed to sneak back into his office while he was in class and delete the video from his computer.

So, HE'D MADE A MISTAKE, Ethan admitted as he drove to the gym Monday evening. An error in judgment. He wasn't perfect. Plus, he was accustomed to getting a good night's sleep. And for the last three nights he'd been kept awake or awakened—or both—by Lily's animals. Or Lily. People tended to make bad decisions when they were sleep deprived.

And having sex with Lily had definitely been a bad decision.

She was dependent on him right now, probably still in shock over losing everything she owned. He was the mature adult here. He should have been more responsible. In some ways Lily was so naive. He should be protecting her. Not taking advantage of her. And the best way to take care of Lily was to get her out of his house.

Because he couldn't guarantee it wouldn't happen again.

What was he thinking? Of course he could. It was simply a matter of willpower.

With renewed determination he stole the ball from his opponent, dribbled it down the court and slammed it into the hoop. He played until his calf muscles screamed and his lungs burned, then he showered and headed home.

Pulling into his garage, he took a deep breath before he got out, turned the doorknob and stepped inside.

The bird squawked and announced that he couldn't handle the truth. The rodent squealed. The old hound got up and headed toward him, wagging his tail, and the black cat wound around his leg, as usual. Ethan gritted his teeth. Chaos.

It seemed there was more stuff cluttering the place— a vase of flowers on the kitchen counter, a patchwork quilt draped over his couch and a couple of potted plants in the empty dining room beneath the window.

But no Lily.

He strode down the hall and listened at his bedroom door. Silence. Maybe she was doing yoga.

Raising his knuckles, he rapped on the door.

No answer.

Maybe she had her earbuds in. He opened the door and peeked in.

Empty.

It was after nine at night. Where could she be?

In the kitchen he perused the fridge, slammed it shut. She was probably looking for a place to live. He paced to the windows in the empty dining room, peered out a moment and then closed the blinds. Maybe she was signing a lease right now.

Scowling, he paced back to the kitchen and rubbed his churning stomach. She should have waited until he could look at her lease agreement. He could've made sure they didn't overcharge her. The woman didn't even have the sense to keep a fire extinguisher handy, and she thought she could just sign a lease after only one day of looking at properties?

The door from the garage opened and Ethan spun to confront her. "Where have you been?"

Lily froze, her eyes wide. "At the animal shelter. I volunteer there on Monday nights."

Ethan blinked. So she wasn't about to pack up and move out? His breathing eased. "You could have left a note."

"Oh." She bit her lip and looked away. "Sorry about that." She was quieter tonight. Where had the warm and bubbly girl from the past two days gone? She was regretting last night, too.

"Listen, Lily."

"It's late." She scooped up the black cat and held it against her chest, avoiding his gaze.

"Lily," he repeated more forcefully.

With a soft sigh, she looked up. "What?"

"How'd it go with your insurance?"

She frowned. "You want to talk about my insurance?"

"I assumed you'd be anxious to file a claim, look for a new place, get back to your life."

She nodded. "I will. I mean, I am. I'm going to."

"So, what did they say? Do they need a copy of the fire chief's report? The—"

"I called my insurance agent this morning," she assured him, sounding so serious. "The claim is going to take several weeks to pay out. I could rebuild, but that would take months. And finding another place I can afford…" She shrugged one shoulder. "I asked Sunny to keep her senses open for the perfect home for me and my shop."

Several weeks to pay out. Months to rebuild. Maybe Ethan could talk her into letting him give her an emergency loan. And she was going to wait around for a psychic to find her a place? He could do better than that.

"What are your square footage requirements? What kind of financing did you have?"

"Um…the shop just kind of came to me when the universe was ready last time, and I let the banker take care of all the money stuff."

"What about product? If you're planning on reopening right away, you're going to need to place an order soon, right?"

"Honestly, I hadn't even thought about that yet."

"Hadn't thought—? Hold on." He moved past her into the kitchen, pulled open the end drawer and grabbed a yellow legal pad and a pen. "We'll make a list of what you need. Then tomorrow, we'll have a commercial agent show us some available spaces. Who's your banker?"

"First National of Las Vegas. You said 'we.' Don't you have to work tomorrow?"

Ethan shook his head while making a list. This was good. This was something he could do to make up for destroying her life. And return his own life to normal. "I'll take a day of PTO."

"So…this would be like, a professional project that we're going to collaborate on?"

That was a funny way to put it, but… "Sure. The important thing is for you to get back the life you had before I came along and burned it down."

Her white teeth gleamed and her dimples showed as she smiled. "I told you, you shouldn't feel responsible for that. It was karma. What will be, will be."

But he *was* responsible. And he couldn't let himself take advantage of this innocent woman again. A woman with an exquisite mouth, that is. And a body that fit perfectly to his. And legs that wrapped around him as he—

"Ethan? Are you all right?"

He slid his gaze from the legal pad to her hands gently stroking the animal. He wanted her touching him instead. But he'd indulged himself too much lately. Lily was a bad influence. In more ways than one.

"I'm going to bed." He winced at that last word. Images of last night wouldn't leave him alone. Her soft skin, the sounds she'd made. He'd never experienced sex like that. Where he'd wanted to hold on until morning.

Luckily, he'd gotten himself under control in time. The weak part of him that felt too much was what had scared her the other night. Those over-the-top feelings had always gotten him in trouble as a kid. Until he'd learned to extinguish them.

When he met her gaze, her cheeks flushed a deep pink. Had she been remembering the mind-blowing sex too? He clenched his teeth and straightened his spine. "Good night." Before he could change his mind, he headed to his uncomfortable futon for some much needed sleep.

But as soon as he got into bed, he remembered he'd forgotten to brush his teeth. The woman had thrown off his whole routine. He lay there listening as the sounds in his condo quieted and she went into his former bedroom and shut the door. Then he silently made his way to the bathroom, turned on the smaller light over the shower, and gathered his brush, paste and floss from the medicine cabinet.

The counter was littered with female stuff. Face wash, lotion, a curling iron, a round pink compact— He stopped with his toothbrush midway to his mouth as he realized they were probably birth control pills.

That sobered him with a hard dose of reality. She was young—way too young for him—and he had no business risking a chance of pregnancy. He was too old and too set in his ways to be good father material.

Hanging over the shower curtain rod were a wet washcloth and two wet bras, one a leopard print, the other a delicate pink lace. He closed his eyes and wondered if this was what it was like to be married. Sharing a space with a woman, having her stuff everywhere.

He'd come close, once, to having a wife. He'd thought Eleanor and he would be perfect together. That they'd both wanted the same things. But in the end she'd wanted something he couldn't give.

He was wiping his mouth on a towel when the door connecting to the master bedroom swung open.

Lily froze when she saw him. Their gazes locked. Her lips parted; her chest rose and fell. She had on the same faded Garfield nightshirt she'd worn the night before. But of course, his undisciplined mind went straight to picturing her in the leopard-print bra, and threw in some matching panties for good measure.

Something in him craved her vitality. Her affectionate nature. He wanted to groan. "Can't you knock?" he snapped.

If he'd slapped her she couldn't have looked more

hurt. Without a word, she turned and headed back into the bedroom.

Aw, hell. He caught her around the waist and pulled her back against his body. "Lily," he murmured in her ear. "I'm sorry."

With a whimper she fitted herself to him and clasped her hands behind his neck.

His palms slid up to cup her breasts as he kissed down the side of her neck. He clamped one arm around her hips and pushed his hardness against her bottom.

"Love me, Ethan," she pleaded.

Like a splash of cold water to his face, her words brought him back to his senses. He closed his eyes. What was he doing? He dropped his hands and got his breathing under control.

Lily straightened, turned around and pressed her cheek against his chest. He could feel her hot breath on his skin. Her long, strawberry-blonde hair clung to her damp flesh and his.

He gently disengaged her hands from his arms and stepped back.

"Ethan, don't stop," she said in a soft voice.

He had to stop. He had to control himself. "I don't think this is good for either of us." He strode across the hall and closed the door, stretched out on the futon and tried to fall asleep.

AFTER ETHAN LEFT, Lily picked up Humphrey and snuggled with him for a long time, petting his long, soft hound dog ears.

What had just happened? Ethan might have acted withdrawn from her last night, but at least he'd satisfied them both first. She wanted him with a desire that would be unhealthy to deny. Her body ached for completion, and her chest ached for Ethan. The look in his eyes had been bleak and sad. The black aura had been strong, the haze of grief thick.

But how could she convince him to let go of his hang-ups? He seemed determined to deny himself anything fun or joyful. She had to find some way to get through to him. Perhaps the universe was already providing a way. Tomorrow they would *collaborate on a professional project*.

6

"THIS SPACE IS twelve hundred and twenty-four square feet and is currently being used as an office and a shop," Nadine, the real estate lady, stated as she pulled up to a strip mall.

Lily hated it.

"The interior of the office is finished, the place has plenty of parking and it's a great location. Just off Highway 95 inside the city limits." She flashed a dazzlingly fake smile.

Ethan stepped out of the front seat of Nadine's Caddy, put his hands on his hips, shoving back his blazer in the process, and squinted against the midafternoon sun. "This place has possibilities." The man had worn a jacket and tie to go look at real estate.

Lily sighed and got out of the car. This was not how she'd envisioned them *collaborating*. He was a total control freak. "Is this property zoned for both commercial and residential?" she asked.

"Well…" Nadine hedged. "I think it may be. When

we get back to my office, we'll have to look that up." When she said "we" she was staring at Ethan.

Lily stuck out her tongue at the woman behind her back.

Ethan saw her over Nadine's shoulder and scowled.

Lily cleared her throat. "How much?"

Nadine finally shifted her attention to Lily. "Well, it's listed at one seventy-five, but I'm sure we can make an offer and probably get it for less." She batted her lashes at Ethan.

Yeah, Lily knew what Nadine wanted. Her aura was bright orange. Lily stepped between her and Ethan, who looked dark and powerful in his civilian clothes, even if they were slightly uptight. She wished she had Sunny's gift. She'd cast a Stay Away spell, Wicca rules or no. And that was *so* not like her. Was this niggling feeling in her stomach jealousy? Or just that she sensed this woman would not be good for Ethan?

Lily drew in a deep breath and exhaled all the negative energies. "A hundred and seventy-five thousand? Ethan, I can't afford that. That's twice what I paid for my shop."

"It's a great location, though." He studied the highways. "Lots of traffic."

"It's just not right for me." Another *not good* feeling, this time about the building.

"But you haven't even looked inside yet." Ethan sounded exasperated. "Will you excuse us a sec?" he asked Nadine, who nodded, pulled out her cell phone and went back to sit in her Caddy.

"Lily, this is the fourth place you've dismissed out of hand. What's going on?"

"I'm sorry, but there's something wrong here. You'll just have to trust me. I'll *know* the right place when I see it."

His jaw muscle worked as he stared at her. "That's what you said about all the others, too."

"Ethan. The first place was a former gas station. The second wanted a million-two."

"I understand you're still feeling the loss of your home. And change is difficult in the best of situations. But you need to keep an open mind."

"My mind *is* open. And my heart. And it's telling me this isn't the place. Something's wrong here."

Nadine negotiated her tight skirt out of the driver's seat and sashayed over to them. "Shall we look inside?"

"Yes."

"No."

They spoke at the same time. Ethan glared at Lily.

She threw up her arms and gave in. "Fine."

The minute she stepped inside, it hit her. Despair. Violence. Death. She shivered and choked back a lump in her throat.

"Lily? What is it?" Ethan put a hand on her shoulder. "You're shaking."

"Something awful. I can feel it." She had to get out. Pushing past Nadine, she shoved open the door and darted back to the Caddy. *Breathe in calm and peace.*

A few minutes later Ethan and Nadine followed her

out. Ethan was studying her as if she'd declared that
aliens had kidnapped her. Nadine was clearly irritated.
Oh, well. This wasn't the first time her sensitivity to
negative energies had made her seem like a freak. It
wouldn't be the last.

"I have one more to show you—" Nadine began.

"Ethan, can we stop for the day?" Lily needed to not
do this anymore for now. She needed lightheartedness,
carefree fun.

He hesitated, but nodded and asked Nadine to take
them back to his car.

Once they'd bidden the agent goodbye—with assur-
ances from Ethan that he would be in touch soon—
and were headed back in the SUV, Lily slumped in her
seat and stared out the window. What a waste the day
had been. Not only had she not found a new place, but
she didn't feel she'd made any progress in lightening
Ethan's aura. If anything, today seemed to have made
it worse.

When she peeked over at him, he was scowling again.
If he hadn't already thought she was a candidate for
the psycho ward, he did now. And trying to explain the
horrible things she'd sensed in that office would only
make it worse.

She was failing him.

IN THE FOUR DAYS Ethan had known Lily she'd never
been this quiet. He'd thought he would appreciate the
silence inside his SUV, but instead, it only made him

worry. When she'd glanced over at him a second ago, he thought he'd spied unshed tears in her eyes.

Guilt squirmed in his gut. He'd thought taking her to look at properties would be appreciated. What had happened back in that office? Why did his every attempt to help her blow up in his face?

"Ethan, look! A traveling carnival. Can we go, please?" Lily straightened in her seat and pointed over to the other side of the highway. Set up in a shopping center parking lot were a big striped tent, a Zipper ride, a roller coaster and a Ferris wheel. The sun was sitting just above the horizon and the multicolored carnival lights twinkled down the midway.

She put her hand on his forearm. "Please, Ethan?"

A carnival? Those were for teens and families. He just wanted to get home, maybe catch a baseball game and work out. But then he turned to look at her. Damn. Those pleading eyes. If he wasn't careful, she'd have him doing yoga. "All right. Just for an hour."

As he passed through the entrance the same unease washed over him as when he'd stepped into Lily's herb shop. What the hell was he doing here? He inhaled the buttery scent of popcorn mixed with diesel fuel unique to an outdoor carnival, and a vague memory from high school materialized. A couple of guys from the football team and their girlfriends. He'd gone with one of the cheerleaders because it was expected. She'd liked him. He'd liked...her rack.

"I'm starving. Let's get a corny dog." Lily grabbed his hand and tugged him all the way to the ticket booth. She pulled a twenty out of her backpack, but Ethan covered her hand and pulled out his wallet. "My treat." Like he was going to let a woman pay his way.

She flashed him her biggest smile and rose up on her tiptoes to kiss his cheek. "What'll we ride first?"

He must be getting used to her because he didn't stiffen at the kiss. More than accustomed to her. He'd liked the feel of her soft lips on his cheek. "I don't do rides."

"Not even the Ferris wheel? Don't make me ride it alone." Her pretty little lips pouted.

"Don't push your luck." Handing her the tickets, he tucked his wallet back into his slacks pocket and scowled. "I'm here."

"Yes, you are." She took his hand again and headed toward a food stand, ordering two corny dogs, two sodas and some cotton candy. When the food was ready, she took her corny dog and drew a smiley face on it with mustard. "Now that the sun's setting it's cooling off. What would you like to do?"

He didn't care. "Do whatever you want."

"Oh, look at the cute squirrel." She hunched down and tossed him a piece of her corny dog. The rodent hesitated and then scampered up and grabbed it. If Ethan didn't stop her she'd take the animal home. And one rodent in his house was plenty.

"Let's hit the midway." He put his hand at the small of her back and guided her toward the games of chance. She was so delicate he could feel her spine beneath her T-shirt. He took his hand away and focused on the various games. Ring toss, water balloon…ah, here was something he could do. Ring the bell.

Handing the carnival man the appropriate amount of tickets, Ethan picked up the sledgehammer, swinging it halfway to test its weight and feel. His jacket was restricting him. He set the hammer down and shrugged out of it, handing it automatically to Lily. Then he loosened his tie and slid it off, and Lily held out her hand for it, as well. She had a gleam in her eye he didn't like. Or rather, one he liked too much.

Retrieving the hammer, he hefted it up behind his shoulder, then put all his weight and strength into the swing. The puck shot up and hit the bell at the same time the spring action base splintered beneath his hammer with a loud crack.

He'd won. But he'd broken the game.

The carnival man started yelling in what sounded like Russian, gesturing at his broken equipment and then at Ethan.

Looking over at Lily, Ethan saw her eyes widen as she covered her mouth with both hands. Had he scared her? Was this just more proof that he was an overbearing hulk who couldn't control his strength any better than his impulses? Then she burst out laughing, bending over at the waist. When she straightened she was still giggling. She tossed her long hair behind her shoulder and pointed at him. "Omigosh, you should've seen the look on your face."

The game operator was still yelling, and Ethan pulled out his wallet and grabbed all the twenties he had left, intent on paying the man for the damage. Lily hurried over and began speaking to the carnival man in his own language. She gestured at Ethan and the man calmed down, and then…she hugged the old guy.

Ethan blinked in awe. Lily spoke Russian? Between her dimples and her smile and the hug, what male could resist? She had the game attendant eating out of her hand—although he still took the money Ethan offered. And then he let her pick from the large stuffed animals *Ethan* had won as a prize.

She chose a pink pig. A pig. And she spoke Russian. Stunned didn't begin to describe how Ethan felt as he handed the man back his hammer, took the pig from Lily and followed her out of the midway.

For several long moments, he just stared at her as she made her way around the Zipper ride and Fun House of Mirrors. When she stopped to buy a funnel cake, he finally found his voice. "Since when do you speak Russian?"

"Oh, I don't really." She waved a dismissive hand as she stared up at the Ferris wheel. "My mom had a boyfriend once from Saint Petersburg. He wanted to learn English so he could audition for this car oil commercial." She shrugged. "My mom was at work, I was avoiding homework…. I only know enough to be dangerous." She offered him a bite of her funnel cake, holding a piece close to his mouth.

Ethan shook his head. Then he changed his mind, swooped in and took the bite, catching her fingers between his lips. Then he caught her wrist and made sure he didn't miss any of the powdered sugar, by sucking her fingers deeper into his mouth.

She stilled, her gaze locked with his. When he released her she moved her hand to his jaw and stroked his cheek. "I don't know any other man who could look so sexy while holding a giant stuffed pig."

She thought he was sexy. First he wanted to toss the damn pig. Then he wanted to take her in his arms and kiss her until she moaned his name. But he didn't do either. He made himself look away and move on. He didn't do PDAs.

She caught up to him and put her arm through his. "So, tell me something I would never guess about *you*."

He thought for a moment, but his mind was blank. He led a boring life. The only thing he did outside of work was… "I have a fishing boat."

She gasped. "Really?"

"Bought it a couple years ago. McCabe uses it more than I do. I've gone fishing a couple of times."

"Oh, Ethan, I love the water. That's the thing I miss the most living in Nevada. The ocean. The faithfulness of the waves returning to the shore, the mystery of the tides and the vastness of the Pacific. So life-giving, you know?" She smiled up at him.

Why had he told her about the boat? Now all he could do was picture her riding with him in it, wearing nothing but a string bikini…. He shouldn't even be attracted to her. She was too young for him, too crazy, too…Lily.

The last of the sun's rays disappeared and the glow

from all the neon lights on the strip was brighter than a full moon. The asphalt parking lot was littered with popcorn and sticky with spilled drinks. They should probably head for the ex—

"I just have to go on the Ferris wheel." Lily tugged at him as they approached the lineup. The ride wasn't very tall, and the open-air, two-seater chairs looked small. He studied the structural components of the rigging, checking for any loose bolts or faulty supports.

He gave it a grudging nod. "It looks safe enough."

"Oh, good. Then you'll ride with me?"

Raising his brows, he said, "I don't do rides, remember?"

"Okay." And she stepped out of line.

"Wait." He caught her arm and slid his hand down to hers. "We don't have to leave. You go ahead and ride." Hadn't he just been thinking they should go home?

Lily stopped and looked at their clasped hands, but she was shaking her head. "I don't want to ride it alone. That's no fun."

Ethan closed his eyes and clamped his jaw tight to keep from rubbing the aching spot in his chest. How could one tiny redhead make him feel like a Greek god one minute and a jerk the next?

"Fine." He practically growled the word. "We'll ride the thing."

Indescribable joy lit up her face. She squealed and flung herself into his arms and squeezed his waist. "Thank you." Her cheek resting against his chest reminded him too much of last night, and what he'd walked away from. He couldn't quite remember why right now.

He handed the operator their tickets and waited until a car swung down and emptied out. Then they climbed in, buckling the old belt around them both. The seat was so small Ethan had to put his arm around Lily's shoulders to fit. Not a hardship. She turned and nestled into him, her arm curled across his stomach.

When the car swung up and around, her grip on his waist tightened and she shivered. He spread his jacket over her.

"I'm not cold," she said into his chest.

He tucked a knuckle under her chin and raised her face to his. "Then why are you shaking?"

Her mouth curved up on one side in a crooked smile. "I'm afraid of heights."

Ethan threw his head back and laughed. "You're crazy." Still chuckling, he looked back down at her. "Cute, but crazy."

She twinkled back up at him. "And you have a gorgeous smile. You should do it more often."

He felt his smile slip. But he was beginning to agree with her on the frequency issue. How scary was that?

The Ferris wheel jerked into motion again, and she gasped and clutched his shirt. Instinctively, he tightened his grip around her. Their car swung as it rose all the way to the top and then stopped, as more riders climbed aboard far below. Ethan liked her clinging to him, her cheek nuzzling against his.

"Lily, why get on a ride like this if you're scared of heights?"

She studied him and her eyes sparkled with excitement. "Then I would have missed this." She pointed to the flashing neon lights of the strip.

He understood. Same reason he climbed in the cockpit every day.

"Isn't it beautiful?" As she gazed at the last of the fading sunset, her body relaxed. "I can't let fear keep me from experiencing life."

Ethan nodded. The wheel moved around, stopping again about halfway down. They sat in silence and watched the sky turn from purple to black, and stars began to twinkle. The air up here smelled of popcorn and fresh grass and—if he lowered his nose a bit—Lily's shampoo.

"So, what else have you made yourself do that you were afraid of?"

Her gaze dropped and she fiddled with a button on his shirt. "You won't believe me."

"Try me."

"That office building. Something bad happened there. Someone died, and not by accident. It was violent."

"How could you possibly know that?"

She shrugged. "I just get a feeling. I could sense the negative energy."

How could he answer that? He believed in what he could see and hear, taste, touch and smell.

"I was about ten when we moved to L.A. I never fit

in at school, but I usually made a few friends who were weird like me."

Weird? He pictured her as a freckle-faced redhead. The new kid in school. Would he have befriended her? The question was beside the point. She hadn't even been born when he was ten. Suddenly he felt really old.

"There was this boy on the bus who bullied my friend because he was chubby," she continued. "Everyone was too afraid to say anything to the jerk. Including me. One day, I decided I should be brave. I stood up, ready to tell him off. Then I felt this hand on my shoulder.

"I turned and the bus driver stood behind me, shaking her head. She said, 'That boy bring his own bad karma.' I didn't know what she was talking about, but the hairs on my arm rose. Over the next months she helped me understand the colors that I saw around people. She told me I had the gift of knowing, and that it was my destiny to help whoever came into my path."

Lily bit her bottom lip, her eyes serious now. "For the first time everything I'd always felt made sense."

Ethan didn't know what to say.

The Ferris wheel started turning and didn't stop again. As they swung round and round, Lily dropped her head back on his shoulder and stared out at the horizon for a while, then looked up at him. "Thank you for riding with me."

Something about the way she was staring at him made his chest ache. That feeling rose again. He wanted her. And it seemed silly to deny himself. He covered her mouth with his and kissed her, hungry for her taste, her touch. For her body entwined with his.

His rule about PDAs be damned.

LILY WAS RIDING A WAVE OF euphoria as she walked into the condo. She had a mustard stain on her T-shirt, and sticky fingers from the cotton candy, and lips that still tingled from Ethan's deeply passionate kiss on the Ferris wheel.

The world had disappeared when his mouth covered hers. *She* had disappeared. Her body had melded with his and they'd become pure energy. Heat had bubbled up from her center and engulfed her as his lips moved over hers. His teeth had nibbled and his tongue had swept in with possessive intent.

His hand had traveled from her jaw down over her collarbone, and hidden beneath his jacket, he'd cupped her breast. Thumbing her nipple back and forth until she couldn't help but writhe in the confines of the Ferris wheel chair. Round and round the ride took them. She didn't know how many times they rose to the top and swung back down. All she knew was a disappointment when it ended, and then an instant anticipation of what awaited them here, back home.

Ethan, on the other hand, had looked guarded, defensive almost, once the ride ended. As if the principal had caught him smoking behind the school. She didn't mind. His aura had lightened to a dusty orange and the blackness had been gone for a while. His chakras had unblocked slightly. This was wonderful progress. She silently thanked the universe for sending that carnival into her path. If he could let loose his inhibitions enough to kiss her like that—in public—then it shouldn't be too hard to make him forget his reservations here tonight.

She wanted to raise her hands in the air and twirl around the living room. But she'd settle for stripping out of these clothes and spending the rest of the evening making wild and crazy love to Ethan.

He shut the door behind her and then stood there clutching his keys as if they were a grenade with the pin pulled. *No sudden moves, Lily.*

"*Squawk.* There's no place like home," Bette said in greeting.

"Yes, we're home, Bette." Striving for nonchalance, Lily went about greeting her loved ones, filling food and water bowls, cleaning out the litter box and putting the towel over the birdcage. "Night-night, Bette."

Ethan had gone into his room to work out. She'd heard the now familiar clanging of weights and the sharp thud of his gloved fists hitting the punching bag. She was aware when the door opened and he headed down the hall to the bathroom.

A minute later the shower door snapped open and closed, and the water turned on.

Okay, so he liked to stick to a routine. That wasn't so bad. They had all night to make love. She could wait.

When Ethan emerged from the bathroom, Lily stood blocking the door to the spare room. So, she wasn't very good at subtlety. She'd tried to be patient. To give him space. But she'd waited long enough. As he approached, she threw her arms around his neck and pressed her lips to his.

But his mouth remained closed and stiff beneath hers. He reached behind his neck, took her wrists and pulled her hands away.

Oh, no. Not again. She wanted him. She needed him tonight.

This wasn't simply about unblocking his sacral chakra anymore. "Ethan. Don't do this again." She tried to touch him but he held her hands away, his biceps bunching with the effort.

"Listen, Lily. I'm thirty-eight. About to retire. Set in my ways. You're at the beginning of…everything. Let's not complicate this any more than we already have."

"Complicate? What's complicated about this? I want you. You want me."

"Are you kidding? Look up the word *complicated* in the dictionary and there's your picture next to it, sweetheart."

"So? We could complement each other. Yin and yang." His fingers were still clamped around her wrists, forcing her hands away from her body. Erotic thoughts of bondage play between them made her pulse skitter. Her nipples responded, and with every breath she became more aware of his freshly showered scent. She was so turned on.

He shook his head. "I like my life simple, uncluttered and well-ordered. I don't want yang."

Her temper snapped. She jerked her wrists out of his grip and backed away. "Coward!" Pushing past him, she stalked across the hall to her bedroom and slammed the door. Ooh, she hardly ever got this angry. It would take hours of meditation and yoga to purge all this negative energy.

He didn't want yang? That was a load of bull. He was scared of the passion that flared between them. Because if he allowed himself to feel such powerful emotions all the rusty locks around his almighty self-control might snap from the sheer force of them. And Goddess forbid if Ethan ever let himself experience any emotion. He'd have to be hog-tied and—

In a flash she knew what she had to do.

7

WITH A START, ETHAN JERKED awake and tried to swing off the bed. "What the hell?" he roared, tugging at his bound hands. Twisting his neck, he looked up and behind him. The rage drained from him and he blinked. "Lily?"

"Yes." She moved around to the front of the futon.

He examined his wrists. She'd tied his hands with his own neckties to the wooden slats of the futon's armrests. The knots appeared to be simple but secure. He looked back at her. "What's going on?" Despite a twinge of apprehension, he strived for calm in his voice. He'd certainly been in much worse situations.

"You listen to me, Ethan Grady." Her hands were fisted on her hips and her feet were planted shoulder width apart. "All that bull about you wanting a simple, well-ordered life? I'm not buying it."

"Lily…" This time he drew out her name like a warning. "Untie me right now and we'll just forget about this."

With a sigh, she folded her arms across her chest. "If I do that, you'll never get to experience this." She slipped under the sheet and blanket and snuggled up next to him, her cheek on his chest and her hand sliding over to play with his nipples. The sensation was like firing up the jet engines in his F-16. But he had to shake this off. She couldn't get away with this.

"Lily!" Giving her his most menacing glare, he jerked at his bindings again. "Are you crazy? Untie me right now or—" A strangled gasp escaped him as she slid her hand beneath the waistband of his briefs to cup his sex. He was semihard and his dick jerked beneath her palm.

"Don't worry. I'll let you tie me up sometime, okay?" She rose up on her elbow and kissed his jaw, trailing kisses down his neck and nibbling into his shoulder a little. "For now, just enjoy."

He drew in several deep breaths, trying to control his body's reaction. But it was a hopeless cause. His only defense now was his mind. Maybe if he placated her… "You're right. Why don't you untie me so I can enjoy you, too?"

She chuckled. "I'm not some crazy psychopath and you know it." She kissed down his chest and circled a nipple with her tongue.

He bit off the string of curse words he longed to spew. "Crazy? More like criminal." His body strained to get loose. Whether it was to shove her off him or throw her under him and shove into her was a close-run thing. He tugged at his restraints again, but the slats held firm.

"Ethan. Don't you want me just a little?" Lily gripped his erection and began stroking it.

His breaths shortened and his body trembled. A gurgling groan betrayed his enjoyment.

"I'll make you a deal. If you're still mad at me when I'm done, I'll pack up and leave." Before he could contemplate accepting that bargain, she sat up, yanked down his briefs and took his cock deep into her mouth. Oh, gods of war and peace. He groaned long and low.

With playful enthusiasm, she swirled her tongue around the head.

"Lily," he moaned. He couldn't think straight anymore. All he could do was feel his body gearing up for explosive completion.

She sucked him a couple more times, then stopped. "Ethan."

"What." He felt completely dazed. Who was this amazing creature? How had he ever gotten into such a situation?

"Are you enjoying this just a little?" She didn't give him time to answer, but went back to pleasuring his cock with her mouth, cupping his balls and playing with them for good measure.

He thought he nodded, but the more he strived for coherency, the deeper she took him into her mouth, the stronger she sucked him in. If he didn't do something soon, he'd lose complete control of his body. He could feel his balls tightening, the pulsing ache in his dick ratcheting up, ready to explode. Against his will, his hips lifted in his own rhythm. His palms stung where he gripped the ties with white knuckles.

"Feeling your inhibitions fly away?" she teased, as she used her tongue to play with his swollen cock head. "Close your eyes if that helps."

"No," he grunted. "I like—" he drew in a sharp breath "—watching you." He couldn't help but admit it. As long as he was tied up, he might as well enjoy it.

And then he'd kill her.

She took him back inside her mouth, deep and strong, and he grunted like a caveman. She worked over him, matching the rhythm his hips set. He was so close.

Then she suddenly slowed her pace, ignoring his attempts to go faster. "Come on, Lily. Please, finish me."

She popped him out of her mouth. "We don't want this to end so soon, do we?"

"Hell, yes, we do!" he protested, so close to climax.

"Just let yourself enjoy it awhile." She smiled, letting her teeth scrape lightly around him.

No. He'd given in, but there was a limit to how much control he'd allow her. While she teased the tip of him with her tongue and stroked him slowly with her hand, he gritted his teeth and plotted his revenge.

"ENOUGH." In one quick move Ethan rose up, captured Lily's hands in a steel grip, tied them together with one of the silk ties and pushed her to her back. How long had he been free? Before she could think, he'd raised her arms and fastened her wrists to the wooden slats behind her. "Let's see how you like it."

Lily smiled. She had a feeling she was going to like it very much. "How long have you known you could free yourself?"

"Let's just say it took longer than it should have." His hands slid leisurely from the knots at her wrists, running lightly down the inside of her arms, pausing at the sensitive skin at the sides of her breasts. The tips of his fingers followed a swirling, teasing path until they finally circled her nipples. "I don't know which you'll regret more—tying me up or letting me get loose." He moved over her, cupped her breasts and lowered his head, then licked her tightened peaks, teasing them with his tongue until she squirmed. Regret? Oh, she didn't think so. This was an erotic fantasy she'd never played out, and she was eager to explore it with him.

"I was—" she gasped as he gently bit a nipple and then suckled it hard "—desperate."

He lifted his head. Resentment and something…tortured shone in his eyes. "Why?"

Guilt slithered to the surface. Should she have been so impulsive? Was she really helping him? "I felt your passion in that kiss tonight. You wanted me. But you're so uptight. You won't let yourself feel things."

"I feel this." He dragged his palm down over her belly and kept going, sliding two fingers between her legs, parting her, stroking her lightly. "You're so soft."

She moaned and moved her hips against him, needing more.

"And wet." He spread her thighs and pushed the two fingers inside her. "Is this what you want?"

"Yes." It was exactly what she wanted at that moment.

His fingers found a rhythm, set a pace. "Is this why you keep meddling in my life?"

She closed her eyes and whimpered. "Oh, yes."

Despite her affirmative, he withdrew his fingers and proceeded to exact retribution for the way she'd tortured him. Her clit was at the mercy of his tongue, lips and sometimes his teeth. He used his fingers and thumb, but only sparingly. Every time she'd get close to climaxing, he'd back off. Lifting her hips, demanding, begging, did no good. She struggled with her bindings, but he hadn't given her the same option of getting loose.

"Ethan." She gulped in air. "Condoms. Under the futon."

He looked up. His eyes narrowed with determination and he shook his head. "I ought to leave you here like this."

"No, please, Ethan." She writhed, close to tears. She was at the edge of her endurance. Desperate for release.

Swiping a packet from beneath the frame, he rose up over her, balancing on one hand while he played with her clit with the other, keeping her on edge. "Look at me."

She choked back a whimper and obeyed, captured by his gray-green eyes.

"You're the most interfering female I've ever met. No one's ever dared do something like this to me."

Lily had never experienced sex like this. Beyond fun and playful. But she wasn't sorry. She'd felt his chakras unblocking, could feel his chi shift. If he thought she'd apologize, he didn't know her at all. She lifted her chin and met his glare with one of her own. "Then it was time someone did."

Exasperation flared in his eyes. He moved between her legs and entered her, shorting out her circuits, her climaxes coming one after another as he thrust inside her over and over.

She stiffened and gasped and cried out. And as her body relaxed and she quieted, his thrusts slowed down. Their gazes met and his expression softened. Propping his weight on his elbows, he stroked her hair and face, and kissed her oh so gently on the lips, down her neck. Then he choked in a breath and thrust hard one last time. He threw his head back and moaned in pleasure, the tendons in his neck straining.

He laid his head next to hers and she felt his heartbeat against her chest, loud and strong and fast until it slowed and his chest quit heaving. The warmth of his skin, the scratchy stubble against her cheek and the beat of his heart were like a drug, and her eyelids grew heavy. Just before she drifted off she wondered if she should ask him to untie her.

ETHAN SAT IN THE conference room the next morning, taking notes at the staff meeting held every Wednesday.

Okay, so he wasn't taking notes. He was pretending to. But he couldn't concentrate on whatever the squadron commander was saying.

He'd woken to his alarm to find himself lying beside a soft, warm body, his arm flung across her stomach. He'd been besieged by a fusion of lust, guilt, shame and wonder. Damned if he hadn't been tempted to take her again before untying her.

But he'd forced himself to get up and resume his usual routine: an hour's run, followed by a shower, and then his customary breakfast: protein bar and filtered water.

When he arrived on base, everything in his office had looked exactly as he'd left it. His schedule for the rest of the day was a routine he'd grown accustomed to over the years. Everything seemed normal.

On the surface.

A part of him thought he might get home this evening and discover last night had all been a dream. In the light of day, with sunshine streaming in the conference room window, what had been done to him last night and what he'd done in return seemed surreal.

But it'd been damn hot. He wished like hell he could deny he'd enjoyed it. But he couldn't.

So much for protecting her, for not getting involved with a crazy lady who believed in auras and chi-whatever. The way he saw it, he had two options. Find an apartment before he got home that allowed pets, and pay the first six months rent. Then move her out and wish her a happy life.

Or he could go home and make love to her all night long.

And maybe tie her up again.

His blood raced south. He pictured her squirming on the futon, her hands tied above her….

You are one sick puppy, Grady.

And that was the crux of the problem. If he let her into his life, would he be able to get her out of it again? Or would she sweep him up into her own chaotic world?

"Lieutenant Colonel Grady."

Ethan straightened in his chair, his attention riveted on his commander. "Yes, sir."

"I asked if your presentation was prepared?"

"Yes, sir."

Hughes was staring at him with a worried expression. Ethan was glad McCabe belonged to a different squadron.

"Well, then, would you mind sharing the latest trainees' test results with the staff?"

"No, sir." Ethan stood and plugged his thumb drive into the overhead PC, and his PowerPoint presentation with the reports he'd spent the weekend preparing flashed up on the screen.

AFTER A LONG DAY, Ethan arrived at his condo, his decision made. He would just have to compartmentalize for a short while. Make sure to separate his real life—his career, his buddies—from his affair. What he did away from the base had nothing to do with who

Get 2 Books FREE!

Harlequin® Books,
publisher of women's fiction,
presents

REE BOOKS!   Use the reply card inside to get two free books!

REE GIFTS!   You'll also get two exciting surprise gifts, absolutely free!

GET 2 BOOKS

We'd like to send you two *Harlequin® Blaze™* novels absolutely free.
Accepting them puts you under no obligation to purchase any more books.

HOW TO GET YOUR
2 FREE BOOKS AND 2 FREE GIFTS

1. Return the reply card today, and we'll send you two *Harlequin Blaze* novels, absolutely free! We'll even pay the postage!

2. Accepting free books places you under no obligation to buy anything, ever. Whatever you decide, the free books and gifts are yours to keep, free!

3. We hope that after receiving your free books you'll want to remain a subscriber, but the choice is yours—to continue or cancel, any time at all!

EXTRA BONUS

You'll also get two free mystery gifts! (worth about $10)

FREE!

Return this card promptly to get
2 FREE BOOKS and 2 FREE GIFTS!

YES! Please send me 2 FREE *Harlequin® Blaze*™
novels, and 2 free mystery gifts as well. I understand
I am under no obligation to purchase anything, as
explained on the back of this insert.

*About how many NEW paperback fiction books have
you purchased in the past 3 months?*

❏ 0-2	❏ 3-6	❏ 7 or more
E9Q7	E9RK	E9RV

151/351 HDL

FIRST NAME

LAST NAME

ADDRESS

APT.#

CITY

STATE/PROV.

ZIP/POSTAL CODE

Visit us at:
www.ReaderService.com

▲ DETACH AND MAIL CARD TODAY! ▲

(H-B-10/10)

The Reader Service — Here's how it works:

Accepting your 2 free books and 2 free mystery gifts (mystery gifts worth approximately $10.00) places you under no obligation to buy anything. You may keep the books and gifts and return the shipping statement marked "cancel". If you do not cancel, about a month later we'll send you 6 additional books and bill you just $4.24 each in the U.S. or $4.71 each in Canada. That is a savings of at least 15% off the cover price. It's quite a bargain! Shipping and handling is just 50¢ per book.* You may cancel at any time, but if you choose to continue, every month we'll send you 6 more books, which you may either purchase at the discount price or return to us and cancel your subscription.

*Terms and prices subject to change without notice. Prices do not include applicable taxes. Sales tax applicable in N.Y. Canadian residents will be charged GST. Offer not valid in Quebec. Credit or debit balances in a customer's account(s) may be offset by any other outstanding balance owed by or to the customer. Books received may not be as shown.

If offer card is missing, write to The Reader Service, P.O. Box 1867, Buffalo, NY 14240-1867 or visit www.ReaderService.com

BUSINESS REPLY MAIL

FIRST-CLASS MAIL   PERMIT NO. 717   BUFFALO, NY

POSTAGE WILL BE PAID BY ADDRESSEE

THE READER SERVICE
PO BOX 1867
BUFFALO NY 14240-9952

NO POSTAGE
NECESSARY
IF MAILED
IN THE
UNITED STATES

he was essentially. Only at night he'd indulge in a brief, imprudent sexual affair.

Anticipation thrummed through his veins. He unlocked his condo door and stepped in, prepared for anything.

What the... Ethan stared around him in disbelief. He never knew what to expect with Lily, but this was even more bizarre than usual.

Scarves were tossed over the lamp shades, leaving the room lit with only a dim, warm glow. Large pillows were scattered on the dark wood floor. There was a faint smokiness in the air mingled with the scent of exotic incense. Soft music filled the condo, a Middle Eastern beat with bongo drums and a flute.

But the best—or worst—thing was Lily. She greeted him on one knee, with her palms together and her head bowed. *"Namaste,* Master."

Master? Ethan's pulse pounded. She was dressed like a harem girl, with a bangle-covered bra, and sheer, loose pants riding low on her hips. A belt made of the same gold and silver bangles as the bra jingled. Her little belly button jewel twinkled and her feet were bare.

"Lily, we need to talk."

"Yes, Master. Your wish is my command." She got to her feet, put her hands to the tie at his throat and started loosening the knot.

Her scent drifted to him and he closed his eyes and breathed it in. The fragrance reminded him of desert nights and sheikhs. "What is your perfume?"

"Bergamot, lavender and sandalwood," she said as she slowly slid off his tie. "Do you like it?"

He breathed in again. "Yes."

She smiled. "Come, rest yourself." Placing her hands on his shoulders, she guided him over to sit in the bean-bag chair. Since he'd decided on this course of action, he let her remove his tie, and sat.

"Would Master like his slave to dance?"

Slave? "Yes," he heard himself answer, as if from far away. She was doing it again. Leading him down the rabbit hole into her fantasy world. He gave up the fight and followed.

LILY POINTED A pink-painted toe and began undulating her hips slowly up and forward, then up and back. Ethan looked the part of the modern sheikh, leaning back with his legs spread, his large hands covering his bent knees and his gaze devouring her inch by inch. Tonight she was his harem girl. Graceful, sensuous, provocative.

She snaked her arms above her head and clanged the finger symbols as she danced. Moved closer until her purple belly jewel was at his eye level. She pulled a scarf from where it had been tucked into her belt and held it over the lower half of her face as she shimmied and shook her hips to the pounding music.

Her heart matched the drumbeat inside her chest. Her skin felt hot where his gaze landed. Her nipples tightened under the heavy beaded bra just from the thought being at his command. But she noticed he wasn't in complete control of his reactions, either. His fists clenched on his knees and, as she moved nearer, he swallowed. Beneath his uniform slacks she could clearly see the outline of his erection straining the fabric. And a sheen of sweat dampened his forehead and upper lip.

Unable to wait any longer, she dropped to her knees and began unbuttoning his shirt. He grabbed her wrists. "If we're going to do this, we should discuss some ground rules."

Rules? She lifted her gaze to his, but she couldn't read his expression. "Did you have fun last night?"

"Fun?"

"Yes." She pursed her lips and raised her brows. "You know, something that is enjoyable, entertain—"

"Yes." He cut her off.

She grinned. "Me, too." She returned her attention to unfastening his buttons, and he didn't stop her this time. "The only rule we need is to stop when it's not fun anymore." She released the last button and dropped her hands to her lap. "Tonight, I'm yours to command." Keeping her gaze lowered, she inhaled a shaky breath and bit her lip.

A moment passed in silence, and she feared he'd tell her to get up and quit acting silly.

"Take off your clothes."

The authority in his voice sent a shock wave of desire straight to her core. She looked up at him and saw the glint of steel in his eyes, the hard line of his mouth. Here was the officer accustomed to commanding a squadron of airmen. How...exhilarating.

Her mouth curved in a seductive smile. "Yes, Master."

She reached behind her and unclipped the belt, then hooked her thumbs in her harem pants, stood and pulled them down her legs. All she wore now was a tiny thong and the bra. She heard his breath catch and he cursed under his breath.

Leaning back in the beanbag, he waved a silent command to continue. The all-powerful sheikh.

She became hyperaware of her body as his intense gaze traveled up her legs, lingered at the triangle of pink material between her thighs, and then moved up to her stomach and breasts. Goose bumps rose on her arms. Her nipples tightened to the point of pain, and her stomach contracted.

"Everything, Lily."

Something deep and primal in her responded to his command. She unhooked her bra and dropped it, then stepped out of her thong.

He made her stand there while he took his time perusing her. The fact that he was still dressed while she was completely naked drove her to the brink of orgasm. She fought the urge to touch herself.

Finally, he unbuckled his belt, unzipped his pants and shoved his briefs down to release his straining cock. "Come here."

Without hesitation she obeyed, straddled his lap and began to lower herself onto him.

"Wait."

She stopped, her hands clenched on his shoulders.

"You have a condom tucked around here somewhere?"

Her stomach fluttered. "Yes, Master." She reached beneath the beanbag chair, produced the foil packet and, at his nod, rolled it down his rigid length. The skin was so hot in her palm, and so soft. The reddened tip leaked a drop of clear fluid.

With a soft moan she sank onto him.

He leaned his head back and closed his eyes.

Lily adjusted her knees beside his hips and pushed down until he filled her to the hilt, then rose and sank again, craving the friction against her clit.

He cupped her breast with one hand, but placed the other at her waist and pushed his hips up to meet her, signaling that he would set the pace. But his dominance didn't feel like role-playing anymore. If it ever had. She untucked his shirt, spread it open and ran her hands over his chest. She adored his tight pecs and the black curls covering them. Leaning down, she placed her lips on his right nipple. He stabbed his fingers through her hair.

With a dominant growl, he clasped her bottom and moved faster, thrust harder. So close to the edge already, she came undone, crying out as tremors of ecstasy broke over her in waves. "Ethan."

"What happened to calling me Master?"

His face was still unreadable. She couldn't tell if he was serious or not. But it didn't matter. She was his tonight. To do with as he pleased. And that thought brought an aftershock of muscle spasms. With a whimper, she closed her eyes and dropped her head on his chest, feeling her passage clench around his still-hard cock.

While she was trying to catch her breath, he stood

and carried her to his bedroom and set her down on the large mattress. Throwing her arms over her head, she lay spent and yet restless, needing him still.

He yanked off his shirt and finished undressing, watching her the whole time. Then he returned to stand over her, took her ankles and tugged her toward him, hooking her knees over his shoulders. She'd never felt so vulnerable, so weak. Even when she'd been tied up last night, she'd still felt powerful. With his fingers he scooped up her juices and played with her clit until she came again and was lifting her hips, begging him to come inside her.

"Ethan, please." She ran her palms over his rippled abs.

A corner of his mouth crooked up. He quickly reached for a new condom and sheathed himself. With infinite control he fitted himself to her and slowly entered her. At first he moved with long, slow strokes, until she thought she would scream. But she could see the tension lining his face and tightening his shoulders. He dropped his weight to one hand and bared his gritted teeth as he thrust harder and faster, his control slipping at last.

When he lowered his head and moaned and pushed in deep one last time, she lost whatever control she might have had and soared into oblivion.

8

LILY CAME SLOWLY AWAKE in a tangled heap on Ethan's bed. Her arms and legs were entwined with his, and they were both twisted in the sheets. It was well past dawn. Humphrey scratched at the door again and she realized that's what had woken her. But she couldn't move yet.

Yesterday morning she'd awoken alone. Today, a delicious happiness filled her inner being that he hadn't left her yet. She would have smiled against his chest, but even that seemed too much effort.

Every muscle in her body ached. Her nipples and clit were sore and tender. But her chi was humming with good energy. Ethan's aura, even in sleep, was a muddied gray. But his face was relaxed, sated.

After making love three times in one night, what man wouldn't be?

This definitely called for a day of playing hooky. Just thinking about spending the whole day in bed with Ethan sent happy tingles all through her body.

But maybe more sleep first. She closed her eyes, luxuriating in the warmth of his arms around her.

Then Humphrey scratched again. She'd forgotten the poor baby.

Afraid the dog would wake Ethan, she slid out from under his arm to let Humph out. But when she moved, Ethan came instantly awake, sat up and shot out of bed.

He scrubbed a hand over his jaw and ran a hand through his hair, then made his way into the bathroom. But he didn't return. She should have known his military training wouldn't allow him to just roll over and go back to sleep. Lily crawled out of bed, grabbed her robe and went to let Humphrey outside. Then she sneaked into the bathroom.

Ethan was stepping into the shower. Lily smiled. Dreaming of him having his way with her under the pulsing hot water, she followed him into the shower and slipped her arms around his neck.

But he scowled, grabbed her wrists and set her away from him. "I'm late for work already."

"Why don't you call in sick and we can spend the day together?"

"I'm not sick."

"I *know* that. I just thought—"

"Look, I have responsibilities. And you should get an update from your insurance agent and continue looking at properties." He turned his back on her and started lathering shampoo into his hair.

Lily stood there a moment, suddenly feeling very

naked. Crossing her arms over her breasts, she stepped out of the shower and grabbed her robe. But she couldn't move. Where should she go? Not back to that bed, the bed that smelled of Ethan and incense and lovemaking. As if in a daze, she wandered down the hall and finally sat on the black sofa, pulled her knees up and hugged them.

The energy emanating from him was once again negative and dull. *Well, what did you expect? That he'd fall on his knees in gratitude and admit he'd seen the light?* So why was she feeling so…dismissed?

Because she'd felt something last night. That same connection she thought she'd felt the first time.

But this project wasn't about her feelings. This was about helping Ethan along his spiritual path to Zen. And if a wild night of fantasy sex hadn't completely unblocked all his chakras, that only meant she needed to discover what would. Ethan needed balance in his life. And she knew deep in her gut that she could help him find it.

He didn't believe in her. But then, Theo had, and she hadn't been able to save him. The instant he'd told her he was being deployed to Iraq, she'd known something bad would happen to him. She'd told him about her "feeling," and he'd come home the next day and asked her to marry him. And kept asking until she'd finally agreed.

Theo had understood that, to her, love was like enlightenment; it was something to be shared with everyone and anyone that karma might send to her. She'd honored Theo's love and belief in her by using her special gift to help others. It was her destiny.

Folding her legs into the lotus position, she placed her hands palm up on her knees, touched each thumb to her middle fingers, and closed her eyes.

Her breathing slowed as she searched for understanding.

Something in Ethan's past was the key to unlocking his emotions. She must get him to open up about his family.

But Rome wasn't built in a day. She needed to remember Sunny's tarot reading. Things would get worse. But they would get better.

Her spirits restored, Lily got up and let Humphrey in, then uncovered Bette's cage. "*Namaste,* Bette."

"*Squawk.* Play it again, Sam."

Lily smiled. "Here's looking at you, kid." She did have a lot to do today. She needed yoga, and a shower and—

Ethan stepped out of his walk-in closet fully dressed, tightening his tie. She glanced behind him. Perfectly aligned matching wooden hangers held starched shirts, pressed slacks and dry-cleaned suit coats and uniforms, all sorted and divided. On the floor was a neat row of shined dress shoes and clean running shoes. Who owned clean running shoes?

Her gaze returned to his. His eyes burned into hers. Where had this come from? He'd been so reserved in the shower. But she didn't need to see his orange-red aura to know he was radiating sexual energy right now.

Flames seemed to lick over her body as he strode toward her, wrapped one arm around her waist and tugged her close. He jabbed his fingers through the hair at her nape and pulled her head back. His lips parted and he took her mouth possessively, then dragged his mouth to her earlobe and softly bit. "I'll be home early tonight."

She moaned, wanting more, but he released her and was gone.

ETHAN WANTED TO LEAVE work at precisely five o'clock Friday evening, but a training sortie and debriefing ran late. By the time he finished the paperwork it was almost seven, and his stomach was tight with impatience to get home to Lily. And yet he resented his eagerness to be with her. It signaled a lack of discipline.

But when he held Lily in his arms he didn't care. About discipline. Or order. Or much of anything except how she felt beneath him, against him. Surrounding him.

He'd never felt this kind of wild, crazy need before. As if he had to be with her, had to lie next to her, feel her skin against his. The past three nights he'd made love like he was eighteen again. Taking her against the wall, on the kitchen counter, and then again, once they made it to the bedroom. Eating in bed, and then making love again. Barely sleeping. His mind knew it couldn't last. But his body craved it more and more.

When he pulled up to his condo, Hughes's Mustang was parked out front. Ethan cursed under his breath.

So far, he'd managed to keep his two worlds separate. He'd like it to stay that way.

He stepped in the door to find McCabe with Hughes. They were both dressed in their dark blue dress uniforms, complete with white gloves, and hats in their hands. Lily was offering them some of her decadent chocolate cake.

McCabe and Hughes turned toward him and saluted.

Returning their salute, he glanced from them to Lily. "What's going on?"

"I stopped by your office to remind you about tonight, but you were still out on a training mission," Hughes explained.

"Tonight?"

"You'd said you'd accompany me to the awards banquet, sir?" She raised her brows.

Damn. "That's tonight?" Hughes was receiving a medal, and he'd committed to going weeks ago.

Lily glanced at him, her big turquoise eyes questioning, as if he'd purposely kept the banquet a secret from her. Which he would have, except he'd completely forgotten it. He never forgot engagements.

If it'd been anyone else asking him for anything else… "Fine. I'll see you there in half an hour."

"Aren't you going to bring your guest, sir?" McCabe asked, flashing his lady-killer smile at Lily.

"She has nothing to wear to this kind of event."

"Oh, I'd love to go."

Ethan and Lily spoke at the same time. Lily's expression was so full of hurt that it made him flinch. Damn it. He clenched his teeth to keep from snarling. "What the hell are you even doing here, McCabe?"

"I offered to escort Hughes if you had other plans." The captain smirked and rocked back on his heels.

Bull. Ethan knew better. McCabe had showed up just to see if Lily was still staying here. And to give Ethan a hard time about it.

"I'm perfectly capable of going alone." Hughes glared at her nemesis.

"No need, Captain," Ethan told her. "Just give me fifteen minutes."

"If you're going to leave this pretty lady here all alone, I'll be glad to take her."

If McCabe didn't stop smiling at Lily, Ethan would make sure the next aircraft his buddy flew would have a propeller. Ethan's mind scrambled for any half-decent reason why Lily couldn't go tonight.

Nothing occurred to him.

"I think maybe I should stay here." Lily shrugged, smiling.

"Well, now, that seems a shame, sweetheart." McCabe broke in before Ethan could speak. "Maybe I should keep you company."

The implied threat earned McCabe deadly glares from not only Ethan, but Hughes, as well. He needed to diffuse this situation before it became a snafu he couldn't repair, Ethan decided. Before he could change his mind, he said, "Get dressed, Lily. You've got twenty minutes."

Throwing McCabe a fierce scowl, he went to shower and change.

HE DIDN'T WANT TO TAKE HER.

Lily's hands trembled so much she could hardly brush on her mascara. She had a bad feeling about this. Maybe she shouldn't go to the banquet, after all. When she'd realized Ethan was embarrassed to be seen with her in front of his colleagues, a strange ache had risen in the pit of her stomach.

Had she completely misread the past few nights? There'd been a gradual change in him. In the mornings, before work, he was still detached and preoccupied, but at night he'd been like a different man. Smiling. Laughing, teasing and, most importantly, not leaving her to go sleep in the other room after making love.

She cherished those times the most. Those brief moments after the orgasmic euphoria, when Ethan seemed to give himself over to her keeping. When he let go of all the baggage choking him, and she felt so close to him. They had seemed one with the universe and each other.

How could her perceptions have been so wrong?

Pulling the vintage satin dress from the closet, she held it up and stood in front of the mirror. Wistfully, she swayed right and left, watching the skirt flare out. There'd probably be music tonight, and dancing. Would Ethan dance with her?

She'd bought the dress on impulse at Goodwill the other day. The tiny multicolored flowers embroidered on the V-necked bodice were so happy and springlike that the dress radiated oodles of positive energy. It'd be a shame not to get to wear it.

And as if she'd known Lily would need them tonight, Sunny had insisted on gifting her with a pair of heels and a delicately crocheted yellow shawl. Surely that was a sign that Lily was supposed to go to this banquet. Perhaps something was meant to happen there that would further Ethan on his journey to peace and happiness.

Decided now, she hurried to finish dressing. She opened a new package of miniature clippies to hold her misbehaving curls on top of her head, sprayed on just a touch of Lily of the Valley, and swiped her lips with Raspberry Pink lipstick. Voilà.

With one last look in the mirror, she felt her insides twist with unease. But she shook it off. What was meant to be would be. Throwing the shawl around her shoulders, she hurried into the silent family room. All three uniformed officers stood as she entered.

Captain McCabe—Mitch—was grinning at her, his gaze sweeping over her from ankles to breasts without ever making it to her eyes. His aura wasn't orange, though. It was a messy, muddied red. He was angry. The kind of anger that weighed a person down after years of resentment.

Captain Hughes—Alex—was looking at McCabe. Her aura was red, as well, but had a faint rose lining. Anger and affection.

A tingling sensation lifted the hairs on the back of Lily's neck, and she looked over to see Ethan staring at her, his eyes taking in every inch of her, deliberately, possessively. His gaze was so intense she could feel his sexual energy like a solid entity slamming into her. Her nipples tightened and a quick jolt of pleasure crashed between her thighs.

Closing her eyes against the tide of carnal forces, she lifted a hand to her warm cheek.

"Are you ready to go?" Ethan jingled his keys.

Inhaling his musky cologne, she smiled up at him.

Opening the door of his SUV for her, he handed her in before going around to the driver's side. He'd done that before, when they went to the pet store and when they'd looked at properties. It was as automatic to him as straightening his tie. But the warmth of the gesture sent positive vibes all over Lily.

Smoothing her skirt beneath her, she slid into the soft leather seat and sank back, feeling safe and tranquil. The Pumpkin got her from point A to point B, but there was something to be said for riding in a luxury vehicle. She felt like a princess going to the ball.

And though she was bound to turn back into the servant girl eventually, she was going to enjoy being with the prince for as long as she could.

It took a few minutes before Lily was cleared and allowed to enter through the security gate at Nellis, after producing her social security number and ID. The banquet was held in the officer's club, and she indeed felt as if she was at a royal ball. Men and women in their dress uniforms, with white gloves and shiny medals on their jackets. White linen and sparkling crystal. Fresh flowers and fine china. The room looked beautiful and hummed with positive energy.

Ethan kept his hand firmly on the small of her back

as he guided her from one group of officers to another, introducing her by name only. Again she felt that safe and cared-for sensation as his palm connected with her spine. Everyone without exception raised their brows to see her with him. An inappropriate pride welled inside her to be with such a handsome, admired man.

Of course, he wouldn't have brought her if he hadn't been forced into it by Mitch.

Speak of the devil. The blond god was swamped by females of every rank, while Alex remained beside Ethan and her.

After everyone took their places at tables, dinner was served, and Lily found herself seated between Mitch and Ethan.

"So, Lily." The captain leaned in. "I guess Grady really enjoyed his massage last week? Ow!"

She glanced down to see Mitch rubbing his leg. She smiled at Alex, who was sitting on the other side of him. "You two must be good friends, for him to let you do that."

"Let me?" Alex's face registered outrage and she folded her arms across her chest. "He's lucky I let myself be seen with him in public at all."

"Hey, what'd I do?" Mitch protested, and Alex glared at him.

Lily glanced at Ethan. Was he feeling that way about her? That he didn't want to be seen in public with her? "Yet when you speak of Captain McCabe your aura is a deep rose. You have great affection for him."

Mitch grinned. "Of course she does."

Alex's eyes narrowed and her lip turned up in a sneer. "All that weirdo outer-dimension stuff is a bunch of bull."

Was the female fighter pilot angry at her for some reason? Lily wondered. "Everyone must choose their own path to enlightenment," she murmured.

Turning her gaze to Mitch, she studied him. "Your fourth chakra is completely blocked. I wonder how I didn't notice it when I first met you." She let her gaze drift over to Alex and back. "But then, Alex wasn't with you that night."

Mitch chuckled. "What's the fourth chakra, sweetheart? Maybe you can help me unblock it."

Ethan scowled. "Cool it, McCabe."

Alex seemed to have grown fascinated by the roast beef on her plate.

"The fourth chakra is the heart's energy center. But, I'm sorry, I don't think I'm the one who can help you."

"Well, what's Grady got blocked? And how come you can help him?"

"I don't need any help," Ethan growled.

"Right now, he's working on his sacral chakra."

They spoke at the same time again.

"The sacral, huh? What's that?"

"Drop the subject, McCabe."

"Ethan, there's no shame in—"

"Damn it, Lily, I said drop it. The commander's about to speak."

A high-ranking officer stepped up to the podium and

began a speech. Air force personnel, already lined up, stepped forward as their names were called, to receive medals.

Alex was awarded the Combat Readiness Medal. "For sustained individual combat or mission readiness and preparedness for direct weapon-system employment," the commander said as he pinned a rectangular ribbon with a silver medal hanging from it onto her uniform.

He stepped back and saluted, and she returned the salute. Then he extended his right hand to Alex and she shook it.

After the medals were awarded, a band started playing and couples took to the dance floor. Mitch asked Lily to dance, and Ethan didn't object. In fact, as she moved around the floor with Mitch, she saw Ethan dancing with Alex.

Mitch was an excellent dancer, and despite the fact that she knew him to be a shameless ladies' man, he was a perfect gentleman.

"If you don't mind me saying, Grady is one lucky son of a gun," he told her.

She smiled up at him. "You and Ethan are good friends?"

He nodded. "I like to think so."

"How long have you known him?"

"Let's see…" He closed one eye and looked up with the other. "I'd just returned from two tours in Iraq…. Almost five years now."

"And you're both confirmed bachelors? Never been married?"

"Oh, I'm divorced. But Grady was smarter than me. At least, I've never heard him mention an ex."

At the word *divorced,* the red aura surrounding Mitch flared. There was much hatred in him on that subject. "So even to his close friends, Ethan doesn't reveal himself."

"Uh, no. Revelation isn't Grady's strong suit." Mitch twirled her around with the flair of Fred Astaire. "But I'll tell you one thing." He nodded at someone nearby. "In the five years I've known him, he's never been less than a perfectionist at work. But this week? He can't tell his ass from his elbow." With a mischievous grin, Mitch twirled her away, and she stepped into Ethan's arms. When she glanced back, Mitch gave her a salute, slapped Alex on the back and walked off the dance floor.

Lily looked up at Ethan and saw a little muscle tick in his jaw. Without saying a word, he folded her hand in his, slid his arm around her waist and rocked from one foot to the other. Pressed against his chest, surrounded by his heat and strength, she felt a lump form in her throat. Something kept happening to her whenever she was in his arms. He made her weak and achy. And a longing came over her—for what, she didn't know.

That unnerved her. Usually, she knew her own mind, if nothing else.

Since he didn't speak, she closed her eyes and laid her head on his shoulder. She breathed in his cologne and savored the feel of her hand in his large, warm one.

He pressed his lips to her forehead and rubbed his

cheek against her hair. She lifted her head to read his expression. He was frowning.

She opened her mouth to say something, but didn't have a clue what words to use.

Then the song ended and he took her arm, led her back to the table and announced that he needed to speak with his commander.

As Ethan stalked off, Mitch arrived with Alex and pulled out Lily's chair for her.

Alex waited with folded arms, but Mitch took his seat without noticing. "Having a good time, Lily?"

Alex glared at Mitch behind his back and sat down.

"It's a lovely banquet," Lily murmured.

Mitch introduced her to the other couples not dancing. "Lily is a mystic who can read auras."

After an uncomfortable silence, one of the wives switched seats to sit beside her, and gave her a kind smile. "Do you read palms, Ms. Langdon? I've always wanted to have my palm read."

Lily searched the dance floor for Ethan, and finally located him on the other side of the room, speaking with a group of older men. He caught her gaze but didn't acknowledge that he saw her. She turned her attention to the kind lady beside her. "As a matter of fact, I do. And please call me Lily."

"And I'm Janice. Jim's wife." She nodded toward a youngish, balding gentleman who smiled at her across the table.

"Well, Janice, hold out your right hand."

After telling her about her long life line, showing her where it intersected with her love line, and how that meant she would have a long and happy marriage, Lily was flooded with more requests to read palms. She read most of the wives' at their table and a few of the husbands', making sure to be truthful, but leaving out the few distressing things she saw.

Soon it seemed word had spread about her, and more people appeared at her table to ask for readings.

Ethan drifted into her peripheral vision. He threw her a dark scowl as another lady sat beside her and held out her palm. But he soon left the room, deep in conversation with a gray-haired man.

The space was emptying, people going home. Lily watched the door where Ethan had exited, but he still hadn't returned. The only other couple at their table stood and said their goodbyes.

"So, I gotta know, Lily." Mitch was leaning too close to her, his breath smelling of alcohol. "You mentioned Grady's chakra being blocked, right? Tell us about it."

"McCabe," Alex objected. "It's none of your business."

He continued as if he hadn't heard her. "I knew a massage would do him good. That's why I suggested it as his payment for losing the bet."

Lily nodded. "Karma brought him into my shop last week. I was meant to help Ethan achieve balance in his life."

"Is that so? How do you do that?"

"McCabe…" Alex spoke his name this time like a warning. "Lily, you don't have to—"

"By nourishing his energy."

Mitch raised his brows and drew closer. "Is that what you call it? I'll have to try that line."

Lily stiffened, insulted. "It's not a line. I've helped several others before Ethan. Once I feel he's attained peace, karma will bring someone else into my life who needs my help."

"So, you're *helping* Grady right now?" Alex's tone was cold, edged with anger. "Is Grady aware that he's just your pet project of the week?"

"You make it sound… It's not like that," Lily protested.

Winking, Mitch squeezed her hand. "I understand completely. A girl's gotta do…" He grinned at her, lifting his eyebrows.

Alex shoved her chair back and stood, staring fiercely at Lily. "Grady's old enough to take care of himself, I suppose. But just remember he's a friend of mine." She turned her glare on Mitch. "Grow up." She spun on her heel and stomped out of the room.

Oh, no. Alex was furious. She thought Lily would hurt Ethan? Lily met Mitch's gaze after the other captain disappeared through the door.

"Geez, she's a downer, huh?" he chuckled, but his smile didn't last.

"I'm so sorry I've upset her."

He waved a hand in dismissal. "No worries. She's

been that way for a while now. Well…" He rose from his chair. "I'm off to try out your idea. Wish me luck."

"Try it out?" Lily asked, but he only waved and sauntered off.

She looked around and realized the room was completely empty. But she still didn't see Ethan. Lily picked up her purse and shawl and made her way out through one set of the large double doors into the foyer, where a few people still stood around talking.

The moon reflected off a fountain in the courtyard. A longing for moonlight and the healing power of water overcame her, and she headed outside. The sound of trickling water soothed her, and a soft breeze played in the warm night air.

Drawing in a deep breath, Lily wandered past the fountain onto the grass, kicking off her heels as she did so. She wanted to spread her arms wide and twirl around until she was too dizzy to stand. But she had a strong feeling that something was wrong. Trouble was coming.

"Lily." Ethan spoke from behind her, startling her.

She spun toward him. *Goddess.* His dark and forbidding scowl pulsed with negative energy. His mouth was a hard, grim line.

"What are you doing out here?" He checked as if making sure they hadn't been seen.

"I…" Somehow she didn't think this was a good time to explain how she drew strength from the moon and water.

"You're shivering." He shrugged out of his uniform

jacket and draped it around her shoulders. His hands lingered on her arms. "It gets cold once the sun goes down. Even in July."

"Thank you." Clutching his coat around her, she swallowed, aching at the sweet gesture. She wanted to press herself against him and feel his arms around her, but he dropped his hands and stepped back.

"You ready to go?"

She nodded. "Where have you been?"

"I told you. I had to speak with my commander."

"You were gone for quite a while."

"So, I should've sat there all evening while you played palm reader?"

"No, I didn't expect... I was just... Oh, never mind."

"You're right. It's late." He took her arm and escorted her directly to the parking lot.

"Wait." She stumbled back to grab her shoes and shawl. He barely gave her time to snatch them up before he grasped her arm again and headed for his car.

She'd sensed trouble coming tonight. And tonight wasn't over yet.

9

ETHAN LOOSENED HIS GRIP on the steering wheel and released a long, deep breath. Lily seemed to grow more worried with each mile they traveled back to his condo.

"I wish you would say something." She spoke in that soft, high voice that had coaxed him into this problem in the first place.

He shouldn't blame her for his bad decisions. "No, you don't."

"Ethan, we need to talk about tonight." She'd started playing with the tassels on the end of her shawl.

"There's nothing to talk about."

"But you're obviously angry at me. And I have no idea what I did wrong."

"I'm not angry. And you didn't do anything wrong." *Except look half my age and read palms and talk like a crazy person and distract me while I'm at work with visions of how damn sexy you are.* "Please believe me."

"If you're not angry, and I didn't do anything wrong,

why did you drag me out to your car like you were being chased by the hound of the Baskervilles?"

"You've read *The Hound of the Baskervilles?*"

She crossed her arms and he felt her steely-eyed glare. "Just because I went to massage school and not college doesn't mean I'm not well-educated."

"I didn't mean it that way. It's just that Conan Doyle's not exactly on the required reading list."

She sniffed. "Exactly my point."

Whatever the hell the point was. He exited the highway and stopped at a red light.

"What happened to upset you tonight?"

Geez, she just would not let it go. How could he have started an affair with someone like her? He'd been seduced. Seduced by her sexy little body and the innocence in her big blue eyes. Drawn to her gentle spirit and cheerful disposition. In a mere three days he'd gotten spoiled to waking up in the middle of the night all horny, and finding what he wanted most lying right there in his arms. A week ago he would never have believed he could sleep with someone invading his space. But he'd somehow grown accustomed to her touch.

The trouble—as usual—was of his own making. He'd let his libido get out of control. He'd learned early that men control their emotions, their emotions don't control them. Not since Annie's funeral had he let himself act so undisciplined. His father's slap that day had knocked such disturbing displays right out of him.

"The light's green."

He blinked at the light and hit the gas.

"Ethan, please talk to me."

And she was doing it again. Making him want to tell her things. "My commander ordered me to take the next week off."

Lily gasped. "Because of me?"

"No." Not directly. "It seems I haven't taken any PTO in over a year. Until this week. That brought it to the attention of my squadron commander."

"Mitch said you haven't been yourself at work."

"McCabe should mind his own damn business." Despite his commander's thinly veiled excuse, Ethan knew it had less to do with using up expiring vacation days and more to do with his subpar performance at work this week. Never in his life had he given less than his best.

"But why is this a bad thing? I'd think having some time off would be nice."

"I didn't ask what you think." The words were out before he could stop them. "Hell, I didn't ask for any of this. From the moment we met, you've pushed your way into my life and messed with my mind. All those animals running around smelling up my place—what kind of whack-job has that many pets? I haven't had a decent night's sleep since you moved in. And are you even looking for a place to stay? Surely there's somewhere you could go…." He pulled into his driveway and closed his eyes. Damn. He hadn't meant to go off like that.

When he glanced at her, she turned her head and

stared out the window. But not before he'd seen the devastation in her expression.

Damn.

Silence reigned as he pulled into the garage. She wiped her cheeks and blinked as she got out of the car. Why couldn't he have controlled his outburst? But maybe it was better this way.

She greeted her menagerie and let Humphrey out. Ethan changed into his jogging shorts and shoes and headed for the track. When he got back, he'd apologize.

But an hour later, when he walked in the door, she was gone. Along with all her animals. Her clothes were missing from his closet, and the plants were gone from the window.

She'd moved out.

THE FOLLOWING AFTERNOON, Ethan swung his racquet, grunting with the effort, and shot the ball full force against the back wall. McCabe returned with a pinch serve. Ethan dived for the other side of the racquetball court and threw all his rage into a CB Pinch shot. The ball bounced off the floor and caught McCabe in the rear of the court, making him rush forward. But he missed the shot. Game to Ethan.

He grabbed a towel and wiped his face and neck as he exited the court.

McCabe wiped his temple on his sleeve. "Geez, Grady. Remind me never to play with you when you're pissed off."

"What the hell are you talking about?" He put a hand to his pounding chest. He was getting out of shape.

"Come on. You were possessed out there. If you don't let her go, I'm never gonna win another game."

"There's nothing to let go." Just because he'd sat around his empty, quiet condo for almost twenty-four hours kicking himself for acting like a fool.

"Grab a beer at Duffy's?" McCabe called out as they headed for the showers.

"Why not?" It wasn't as if he had anything else to do tonight.

Once they'd settled on a couple of stools at Duffy's bar, McCabe ordered two Millers and Ethan reached for the bowl of pretzels.

"Okay, so Lily's hot. But women like her are a dime a dozen." McCabe wasn't going to give up. "Seriously. You're starting to scare me."

Ethan took the beer from the bartender. He studied the brown, frosty bottle, remembering how Lily had questioned his abstinence. He had nothing against alcohol in general. He'd had his share of drunken nights in his youth. Letting off steam with the guys after a grueling day of training. But he'd decided after a few hungover mornings that a drunken Ethan was too sentimental, too…emotional.

He raised the bottle to his lips, took a swig and swallowed. "You ever get lonely, McCabe?"

"Me? Hell, no." McCabe took a long pull on his beer. "I have buddies like you."

"You've been married. You don't miss that…companionship?"

His friend set his beer down and turned on his stool to stare at him. "Like I miss a bad toothache. What's got into you?"

"Hell, I don't know."

McCabe gestured with his beer bottle. "Look around. I can find you half a dozen women right here. Women prettier and just as fun as what's-her-name."

Ethan nodded, but McCabe was missing the point. "I just…shouldn't have left it the way I did."

He snorted. "Jackson said you were a sappy drunk back in the day. But you've barely touched your beer."

Ethan raised a brow. "Don't worry. The night is young."

"Well, I wouldn't worry about how you left things with her. She's probably already moved on." McCabe took another draw off his beer. "Believe me. Women have no qualms about loyalty."

Had Lily moved on? Why wouldn't she? She was young and wild and gorgeous. And Ethan had been a jackass. She'd probably slam the door in his face if he tried to apologize now. He set the beer down, took out his wallet and threw down enough bills to cover both beers. "I gotta go."

LILY MADE HER BED on Sunny's sofa, lay down with a sigh and stared at the shadowed ceiling. Her body ached. She'd forgotten how exhausting it was to do one massage after another all day. She hadn't liked working at the

Monte Carlo the first time around and starting today at the big luxury casino hotel just confirmed that it hadn't gotten any better.

But the negative energy surrounding her had nothing to do with her new job. She'd tried to rally, to accept whatever the universe had in store for her. But it was hard to not feel like a failure. After an hour, she gave up trying to sleep, pulled out an astrology magazine and started flipping through the pages.

She should be looking for an apartment. Sunny could take all her animals for only so long. That's why Lily hadn't wanted to stay here in the first place. Of course, she'd had another reason….

When a sharp knock sounded on Sunny's front door, the magazine went flying and Lily literally jumped off the sofa. Peeking first through the door's spy hole, she unlocked the door and opened it a crack. "Ethan?"

"Lily. Did I wake you?"

Her heart started thumping as if she'd just run a 5K. He was actually here. Standing at her door, well after midnight. Did he miss her? Was he going to ask her to return?

After a second of being lost in his light green eyes, Lily opened the door wider to study him. He was wearing jeans and a black T-shirt. The streetlight hit him at just the right angle, causing more than a few strands of gray to shimmer in his short black hair. The shadow of a beard accentuated the masculine shape of his lips. Though his body was rock hard, the creases around his eyes gave away his age.

The casual look was sexy as hell on him.

He held up a key ring with a plastic floater attached. "Want to go fishing tomorrow?"

She blinked and leaned forward. "Have you been drinking?"

"No. Well. Yes, but— So, do you?"

He was going to take her out on his boat? She supposed this was his way of apologizing. But she'd been doing a lot of thinking, and he wasn't the only one who needed to apologize. "I'm sorry I was so...intrusive."

He shook his head. "I was out of line."

Happiness spread from Lily's center throughout her body, and she burst into a smile. On tiptoe, she threw her arms around his neck and kissed his cheek. "I've missed you so much."

He looked down at her, so serious. Then he cupped her face between his palms and kissed her back. A deep, possessive, bone-melting kiss. His body radiated heat and he smelled so fresh and clean. She whimpered with longing and fell back against the open door. Ethan followed, his hands flattening on either side of her head, and pressed his erection against her hip. He pushed his tongue in and moved his lips over hers until her mouth completely surrendered.

When he raised his head, she couldn't quite catch her breath. She wanted to strip him naked, drag him into the house and onto Sunny's sofa. But she needed to check her impulsiveness.

"So," she said, and her voice quavered, "is it okay if I don't actually fish?"

Finally, *finally* he smiled. The flash of his white teeth and the curve of his beautiful lips made him even more handsome. "You can do whatever you want."

What an offer. There was one more thing she'd need to replace…. "I'll have to get a swimsuit."

He stopped smiling. His gaze intensified as it flicked down her body and back up. "Make it a bikini."

THE VIBRATION OF THE 250 horsepower motor rumbled through Ethan's body as he opened up the throttle and let her loose across Lake Mohave. She was a Z19 Comanche bass boat with all the bells and whistles: a trolling motor, a recirculating aerated live well and a three-bank battery charger. He'd forgotten how much he loved the feel of the wind in his face and water spraying over the bow. Why hadn't he taken his boat out every chance he got?

"I love it!" Lily called out, her arms raised over her head as they skimmed over the water.

He glanced at the beautiful redhead sitting on her knees in the seat beside him. Her eyes were closed, her head thrown back, and her long curls danced in the wind. She was wearing an aqua-green bikini that matched her eyes, and she hadn't even bothered to cover up with shorts or a shirt.

He'd been rock hard since daybreak.

And the hell of it was, he didn't mind. He found he was smiling right along with her. After spending the past week or so with a sense of vague dissatisfaction with his life, he was beginning to think maybe having fun wasn't the waste of time his father had always claimed. It was a beautiful day; Ethan had a beautiful woman in his boat. All he needed to make the day complete was to hook a huge striped bass....

He skimmed across the lake, letting his mind wander. Lily had kissed him very primly last night and he'd gone home alone—and frustrated—like a young kid after a first date.

"Where are we going?" she shouted over the engine's roar.

He cut the throttle back. "The guy at the marina told me about a good spot for finding bass. It's marked on the chart." He held the map of the lake out to her.

Lily studied it. "The spot looks like a secluded cove. Are you planning to seduce me, Mr. Air Force Guy?" She threw him a sultry-eyed look and then spoiled the effect by wiggling her brows.

"Absolutely." He scanned the lake for any close traffic and, finding none, turned his attention to scanning her mostly uncovered body. Her skin was creamy-white and he itched to run his hands over every inch. He might not do any fishing, either. "You don't want to fish?"

She shook her head. "I'm a vegetarian. I just couldn't. But I don't want to stop you. I brought a book." She dug into the most humongous woven bag he'd ever seen and produced a thick paperback with a bare-chested guy on the cover.

"You can read Conan Doyle and then that?"

"They're both well-written genre fiction. Have you ever actually *read* a romance novel?"

"I'll take your word for it." Ethan pulled back the throttle and let the boat coast to the right into an inlet, then he cut the engine. "Here we are." He stood, climbed to the front and dropped anchor.

"Oooh, a beach. Are we going to eat our picnic lunch over there?"

He glanced at the rocky shoreline and sparse vegetation. It sure as hell wasn't the Riviera. There was one tall cottonwood tree, but mostly just scrub and a couple of yuccas. "Sure."

While he opened the front compartment and pulled out his fishing rod, tackle box and bait, Lily took a wide-brimmed hat from her bag and a bottle of sunscreen. She plunked the hat on her head and then squirted the thick white cream into her palms.

Distracted by her slathering on the sunscreen, he found it took three tries before he got his lure tied. He wiped his temple on his T-shirt sleeve and squinted at the cloudless sky. The sun had cleared the craggy rock formations of Eldorado Canyon only an hour ago, but it was already warm. By noon it would be over a hundred. Average temps for July in Vegas.

He cast his line off the starboard bow and sat back to wait.

Lily opened the insulated compartment, dug out two icy bottles of water and handed him one.

"Thanks."

She smiled, then leaned back in her seat and opened her book.

Birds circled overhead. A few jets from the base

screeched across the sky. Funny, normally he'd be up there with those pilots, looking down on the lake below. Yet right now he felt not one pang of envy. He reeled the line back in and cast again.

He kept expecting Lily to start chattering about her animals, or tell him some unusual story. Was she actually going to just sit there and read?

Wait a minute. Did he miss her chatter? Her stories? He always fished alone. Came out here on purpose to be alone. He was a solitary type of guy. But the thought of coming home to an empty house from now on was... unsettling. He'd liked having someone there.

Relaxing into the companionable silence, he reeled in his line and cast it back out. Time ceased to matter. How long had it been since he hadn't stuck to a strict schedule? Years? Decades? He reeled in, he cast out.... His thoughts wandered.

He'd camped with his dad once. Before Annie got sick. He must've been five or six. They'd hiked up into the Black Mountains and pitched a tent. His dad had caught a fish and taught him how to clean it. Told him about his Cree blood. Ethan had almost forgotten about that. What do you know? A good memory of his father.

"Ethan, I've just got to cool off." Lily stood and tore off her hat.

Before he could comment she stepped to the boat's edge, pinched her nose shut and jumped off the port bow. A few seconds later she emerged from the water, her hair plastered to her scalp. "Oh, this is wonderful. Come swim with me."

"Lily. You may find this hard to believe, but the bass probably won't bite with you swimming around."

"Doesn't seem like they're biting, anyway." She stuck out her tongue and gave him a mischievous grin.

Damned if he could work up any real irritation.

All he could think of at the moment was having her in his arms in the cool water. He'd never done it in water. Or on a beach, for that matter. A little cooling down wouldn't hurt. Without another thought, he reeled in his line, stored his rod and yanked off his T-shirt.

"Watch out." Aiming for a foot from where Lily swam, he took two steps back and cannonballed in right next to her. He heard her screech just before he hit the water.

As soon as his head cleared the surface she pushed him back under. Didn't she know who she was messing with by now? Standing in shoulder-deep water, he caught her ankle as she tried to escape. She screeched again and kicked out, but he gripped tight and dragged her to him.

Laughing and squealing intermittently, she fought being captured, trying to wiggle out of his arms, but she didn't stand a chance. He held her squirming body against his, an arm around her waist, a hand cupping her firm butt. Her breasts were crushed to his chest and he stifled a groan of pure lust.

With a sigh she gave up the fight, threaded her fingers through the hair at his temples and kissed his eyes, then his nose, and finally his lips. She tasted of herbal tea and fresh mint. He hadn't thought it possible to be more aroused than last night, but even in this cold water, his body responded with enthusiasm. Her hand sneaked down his back to squeeze his butt, and then she pinched him. Hard.

"Ow," he half growled, half yelled. "You want to play rough?" He lifted her by the waist and tossed her into the water. She barely had time to scream before she sank. But she didn't surface. Yeah, he knew this old trick. He folded his arms and waited. And waited.

Still, he wasn't falling for it. He gave it a few more seconds, searching the surface of the lake for air bubbles or ripples.

He was just about to dive under when he spied her sneaking out from behind the boat and swimming for shore.

"Well, I guess she drowned," he called loudly, then swung around and caught up to her with a few powerful strokes. With a squeal she tried to outswim him, but he had more traction in the shallow water. He caught her around the waist, threw her over his shoulder and carried her up to the beach.

Like a pirate, he hauled his laughing, kicking booty over the rocks and headed for the shade of the cotton-wood. Before he set her down, he smacked her on her sexy butt. She yelped and rubbed her behind, then closed her eyes and sank down onto the sandy grass.

He was breathing heavily. So was she.

She smiled up at him, her hair wet and straggly, her

string bikini clinging to her body, accentuating the nakedness of the rest of her. Her coconut-scented sunscreen lingered on his shoulder and reminded him of his fantasy the night he'd met her.

Damn, it was almost déjà vu.

He fell to his knees beside her and ran a hand slowly up her bent leg and down her thigh, amazed at how soft and smooth her skin was.

She held her arms out to him. "Make love to me, Ethan."

"Your request is my command." He smiled sweetly and reached inside his black swim trunks to a mesh pocket and pulled out a couple of foil packets.

She chuckled and he lowered himself above her, his hands braced on either side of her face. For a moment he just stared into her eyes, and then he kissed her, claiming her mouth. She opened to him, teasing him with her tongue while her fingers dug under the waistband of his swim trunks and pushed them down.

"No." He seized her wrist and pushed it to the grass by her head. "We're going to take it slow."

LILY WANTED TO PROTEST, but she could see the resolve in Ethan's eyes. This time when he brought his mouth back to hers he barely touched her lips. With infinite patience he moved his mouth over hers, softly, seductively, as if he had all the time in the world to spend just exploring it. She'd never been kissed like this—a deliberate worshipping of her lips and tongue.

By the time he finally dragged his oh so skillful lips

down her jaw to lightly nip and lick along her neck, she'd melted into the warm earth at her back. Her skin sizzled and tingled all at once as he caught her earlobe between his teeth in a gentle bite.

While his mouth worked its way to her shoulder, he moved between her legs, and his hand skimmed along the inside of her thigh to her hip. He slowly untied one side of her bikini bottom, and his palm flattened over the sensitive area beside her pelvic bone. She shifted her hips to encourage him to go lower, let him know she needed more, but his hand skittered away to caress her ribs.

Since he'd released her wrist, she took advantage of her freedom by running her palms along his massive, straining biceps and triceps. The masseuse in her appreciated his muscles. The woman in her was enthralled with his strength. He could overpower, could crush, yet he was so tender. She caressed his taut pecs with their hard nipples and slight dusting of dark hair. So utterly masculine.

His body was the result of a disciplined regime, and she admired that about him. Had from the first moment she'd laid eyes on his magnificent form lying on her massage table. Every muscle had been worked, no tendon forgotten in his pursuit of perfection.

If yoga was the union of mind, body and spirit, Ethan's commitment to physical fitness held its own brand of reverence for health and well-being.

He pressed light kisses down her arm to the inside of her elbow and back up along the underside of her arm to her breast. He untied her bikini top and pulled it down.

His moist lips teased all around her breast, his hand cupping and shaping it. She enjoyed his unhurried love-making, but he didn't touch the puckered tip that so craved his attention. She couldn't stand it much longer, but she was determined not to beg or whimper. After missing him desperately, she wanted to just enjoy.

He'd taken his sweet time pleasuring her before. But today felt different. Today there was something unfath-omable in his eyes and in his touch that felt more like a connection of souls. Every few moments he would raise his gaze to hers. She saw that depth of feeling.

No words were needed. The only sounds were an occasional moan of pleasure—both hers and his—and the soft lapping of water against the boat's hull.

But the silence was broken with her sharp cry when his mouth latched on to her tight nipple and suckled.

Shifting his weight to his elbows, he pulled the other side of her suit down and cupped her other breast. As if they were his own personal playthings, he pushed them together, caressing them as his tongue flicked the tip of one, then the other, and again, back and forth until his lips settled on one and drew it deep into his mouth. Deli-cious torture. She writhed beneath him, lost in a sensual dream. The world was reduced to only her flesh in his mouth. To her sandy hands massaging his shoulders, gripping his head, digging into his scalp.

Then his mouth left her nipples wet and aching as he moved down, kissing her ribs and her quivering stom-ach, nuzzling into her belly. He gripped her waist and nosed under her bikini bottom, uncovering her smooth pussy. The same thoroughness he'd applied to her mouth he now gave to her core.

His fingers and tongue played with her folds, teased at her opening, taunted her clit. But again, she sensed that this time his intention seemed less about revenge or games, and more about adoration.

As that realization struck she came deeper, harder, longer than she ever had. She squeezed her eyes closed as shudders rocked her. "Ethan."

The orgasm was the first of several. He pulled off his swimsuit and entered her, slowly, intentionally drawing out the sensation. His muscles bunched as he thrust; his body surrounded her, was a part of her. And when he finally came, he gasped, his breath stuttering against her lips.

Eventually the world around her came back into focus. Leaves rustled in the breeze, planes flew overhead, another boat motored by somewhere out on the lake. Ethan moved his weight off to her side and she curled against him, her head on his chest, her leg over his. He scrubbed a hand through his hair and then bent his arm behind his head and closed his eyes. The fingers of his other hand ran lightly up and down her arm, and then stilled.

Lily moved her hand over his heart, savoring this total oneness with him. An energy hummed between them, full of life, harmony…peace. She could get used to this.

She was going to savor the memory long after they'd both moved on.

EVEN DROWSY AND DOZING, Ethan was aware of Lily's foot sliding along his calf, of her hand caressing his chest. Sated as he was, he could feel the stirrings of arousal. Damn, he'd turned into a dirty old man lately. In a minute he should get up and fetch the beach towels and some food from the boat. Then maybe after they'd eaten…

"Ethan?"

"Hmm?"

"I got my old job back at the Monte Carlo."

He opened his eyes and turned toward her. "You worked at a resort?"

She nodded. "For a while. It's good money. And I need to rent an apartment until the insurance pays out."

Instinctively he tightened his arm around her. The thought of spending time all alone in his condo… "You could…move back in with me—if you want," he said with a casualness he didn't feel.

She rose up on her elbow to look at him. "You really want that?"

He brought his hand from behind his head to cup her breast to rub his thumb over her nipple. "We're just starting to get along."

If he hadn't been watching her so closely he might have missed her flinch. She sat up and reached for her swimsuit, started shaking out the fabric.

What the hell? He sat up and grabbed his trunks. Why had she gone so cold and distant all of a sudden? Because he'd suggested they got along sexually?

This, from the woman who'd used his neckties to seduce him?

"You've been so sweet." She tied on her bikini top. "Putting up with my animals." She stood and busied herself brushing off grass and dirt. "And me and all my craziness." Finally, she tied on the bottom. "But I don't want to impose any longer."

Staring at her back, Ethan had no idea what to say to that. He stood, stepped into his suit and yanked it up. Women were the most illogical, perplexing... He clasped her shoulders to have her face him. "I said you could come back and I meant it. I'm getting used to your menagerie."

She grinned. "Even Rhett?"

"Well, now, Rhett may have—"

She cut him off with a light, playful shove to his chest. "I'm hungry. Let's get the picnic basket." She spun on her heel and raced out into the water. "I hope you like cucumber and hummus wraps."

Ethan pretended to groan.

10

WHAT THE HELL HAD THEY put in the water around here lately?

Whatever it was, Mitch decided he'd stick to beer. Shaking his head in disgust, he took a long pull on his bottle of brew and then chalked his cue stick.

Across the pool table, his buddy, ex-air force major turned Las Vegas cop, Cole Jackson, couldn't keep his hands off his new love, Jordan. Bad enough their affair had cost Mitch thirty days of celibacy, but to add insult to injury, they'd actually shacked up together. And the way they looked at each other… Ugh. Mitch rubbed his stomach.

And now Grady? Getting back with that masseuse? He was making a fool of himself over the ditzy redhead. She was nearly half his age. What the hell could they possibly have in common? Somebody sure had a strange sense of humor.

"I don't know how much longer I can watch this,"

Hughes murmured as she stepped close to Mitch, her look of distaste focused on Grady and the redhead.

Good ol' Hughes. He knew he couldn't be the only one in this city of sin to see that Grady had gone over the deep end. "I'm sorry I chose that herb shop now. I figured one sweet night…"

"Maybe it's just a hot and heavy fling." Hughes gathered the pool balls and dropped them into the triangular rack.

"Maybe." Mitch leaned on his stick and rubbed the stubble on his jaw. "But he's been with her for weeks now."

It'd taken an invitation from Jackson to get Grady to come to Duffy's tonight. Jackson didn't have many nights off since he'd hired on with the LVPD.

"McCabe, are you playing pool or looking for your fortune at the bottom of your beer bottle?" Grady barked.

Mitch shoved his beer at Hughes and eased the rack off the balls. "Hughes and I are gonna whip your butts, no disrespect intended, sir." He raised a brow at Grady, bent over the table and positioned his cue.

With a loud whack, balls scattered across the table and the twelve dropped into the corner pocket. "Stripes."

He proceeded to sink four more striped balls before finally scratching.

"I don't know why we bother playing against you, McCabe," Jackson moaned. "You obviously had a wasted youth."

But Mitch didn't feel too sorry for the guy. Jordan

was giving Jackson a consolation kiss before he took his turn at the solids.

How much of this crap was he going to have to watch just for a game of pool? He turned to the other happy couple. "So, how's your chi doing now, Grady? Has Ms. Zen unblocked all your chakras?"

If looks were an air-to-ground missile, Mitch would be dead. Grady tightened his arm around Lily's waist as he glared at him. But Mitch had to give her credit; the little redhead didn't take offense.

"I understand your anger and mistrust, Mitch." She looked up at Grady and cupped his cheek in her palm. "Ethan is your friend and you're worried that I'm brainwashing him into believing in some kind of spiritual mumbo jumbo, right?"

"Actually, no." Hughes spoke up from beside Mitch, shoving off the wall to circle the table. "It's just that McCabe can spot another *player* from a thousand feet." Stopping a foot from Grady and Lily, she cocked her head and folded her arms.

"What?" Lily seemed genuinely confused, and Grady's dark expression grew even more threatening.

Mitch didn't like the insult to himself, but Hughes was a friend, and friends had each other's backs. He rushed to step between them. "Hah, Hughes." He laughed and slapped her on the back, shoving her out of the line of fire. "Since when has Grady ever even pretended to be as good a player as I am?" He leaned toward Grady, as if they were sharing a private joke. "She's just jealous. I'll take her to cool off." And before he could respond,

Mitch quickly grabbed Hughes's arm, dragging her away from the pool tables.

"Geez, Hughes, you got a death wish?" Mitch said as he tugged her along. She tried to jerk her arm out of his grasp, but he tightened his grip and led her onto the dance floor. Elbowing his way through the crowd of dancers, he pulled her into his arms and started two-stepping to a local band's version of Brooks and Dunn's "Neon Moon."

Duffy's was busy tonight, not surprising on a Saturday. A live band played instead of the usual DJ. Cowboy boots shuffled on the polished wood floor and a disco ball reflected a couple of spotlights into millions of colored stars.

"What are you doing?" Hughes spoke between gritted teeth, but she two-stepped in perfect rhythm with him around the dance floor.

"I'm saving your ass. What's it look like?" He took her hand and twirled her under his arm to the two-step beat, and she matched his steps as if they'd practiced the move for days.

"I don't need you to save me, McCabe." She fitted right back into his arms and her baggy camo pants brushed his jeans. He looked down into her defiant eyes. She was pretty light on her feet considering she wore her steel-toed combat boots.

"You got one hell of a temper on you. It's a wonder you've survived this long." He paused, noticing how their hands were clasped together. Hers looked so small in his.

"As lame as your excuse to Grady was, I know what you were doing with him. I meant, why are we dancing?"

"Uh...we already had drinks and I needed an excuse to get you away?"

"We've never danced together before." She gave him a strange look.

He scoffed. "Sure, we must have. Remember that night in Fort Worth? We went to Billy Bob's?"

She shook her head. "That was Luanne."

Mitch stiffened. Even now, eight years later, just her name had him fuming. And for the thousandth time he wished he hadn't been such a pathetic sucker. Or at least hadn't rushed into marriage thinking he was "in luv." What a crock.

Hughes had tried to warn him at the time, but he hadn't listened. Any more than Grady would listen to her tonight.

The song ended and the band started playing a slow, romantic ballad. Mitch and Hughes stood awkwardly, unmoving as couples swayed around them, and then he circled her waist, drew her closer and rocked from foot to foot.

Her oversize T-shirt hid a slim waist. She could bench-press seventy pounds, so he'd never thought of her as small. But the top of her head barely reached his chin.

The band singers were imitating McGraw's and Hill's famous duet about love sending a shock right through them. Mitch was about to make a joke about love sending a shock, all right, a shock of lawyers' bills. But she was staring off into the crowd and all he could see was the top of her backward ball cap. Which smelled like car oil.

Which reminded him… "How's the 'Stang running?"

She brought her gaze back up to his. "I need to rebuild the crankshaft and I'm looking for new connecting rods. But she's running." Her face was so close he could see the freckles on her nose even in this dim light.

"Didn't you just have that crankshaft rebuilt?"

"When I first bought it. That was right after we met, McCabe. Almost twelve years ago."

Back when they were both wet-behind-the ears cadets at the Air Force Academy. Damn. They'd known each other a long time. And she didn't look a day older than when he'd changed all her underwear out for men's briefs their first week of camp.

The song ended and she dropped her hands and stepped back. She turned to leave the dance floor, but he grabbed her arm.

"Hughes. Let's find us some hookups for the night and get out of here, like we used to in the old days." He grinned.

Instead of agreeing as he expected, she got another weird look on her face, as if he was some clueless jackass. "We should get back to Grady and Jackson. We left them in the middle of a game." She pulled her arm from his grasp and threaded her way back to the pool tables.

Damn. What had he done now? He'd thought it might be McCabe and Hughes against the world again. But now he was beginning to believe things would never be the same.

ALEX TRIED TO SQUASH her temper as she headed back to the pool tables. Mitch actually thought she was going to help him find another one-night stand. She looked down at her trembling hands. Damn it.

Being in Mitch's arms just now had all but melted her usual shield. With his chest pressed against hers, and his legs and hips moving to the beat between her own, she'd wanted to lean into his strength and breathe in his scent.

She knew he didn't see her as anything but another good buddy. A pal. And really, with the way he'd been acting since his divorce, that was just as well.

The only problem was, she remembered what he'd been like before. And she wanted that man back.

Damn. She supposed she should apologize to Grady. All right, to Lily. But she just couldn't shake the feeling that Lily was bad news for Grady. Hell, the strange girl had flat-out told them at the banquet last week that she was only sleeping with Grady because she felt sorry for his poor blocked chakras or whatever. And as soon as she was done "fixing" Grady she'd be moving on.

Trouble was, Alex didn't think Grady had any clue that was Lily's plan. The masseuse had gotten her tentacles into Grady's life. He'd been miserable because of this woman. That was unheard of for him.

Alex could see it in his eyes. He was falling for the palm-reading weirdo. And Alex had already watched one good buddy's mental health be sliced to pieces after he was caught in the talons of a deceitful woman.

"There you are!" Jackson greeted her as she approached the pool table.

"Sorry. I was in the can," Alex answered. "Whose turn is it?" She leaned around Jackson's wide shoulders. Lily was bending over the pool table with Grady behind her, his arms wrapped around her, showing her how to hold a cue stick. He wore this goofy, lovesick smile and whispered into her ear. Alex had never seen him like this.

"When you and McCabe didn't come back, we decided to teach our gals to play." Jackson smiled at Grady and Lily.

"Your 'gals'?" Alex's stomach roiled. "Where's Jordan?"

He raised a brow. "You didn't see her in the can when you were there?"

Alex scowled and shifted her gaze over to Grady and Lily. "Do you think Grady's serious about her?" she asked.

When Jackson didn't answer, Alex glanced at him. He was eyeing her suspiciously. "I think she's the best thing that's ever happened to him. What have you got against her, Hughes? You aren't really jealous, are you?"

She snorted. "Come on, please." She shook her head. "Not even."

"Then what's the deal?"

Alex sighed. "Before I say anything, I owe it to Grady to tell him first."

"Well, if it's something serious, you better do it quick."

"Why? What do you mean?"

Jackson's gaze returned to where Grady was "teaching" Lily the intricacies of positioning the cue stick by nuzzling her neck. "He's been asking me how I like civilian life."

"What?" Panic settled in Alex's chest. "You think he'd give up his career for her?"

"He's got twenty years already," Jackson replied. "He could retire tomorrow and no one would blame him."

Retire? No way. Grady could go all the way to full colonel if he stayed in. Maybe even higher. Was that little witch trying to trick him into giving up the only thing he'd seemed to live for since Alex had known him?

One thing was for sure. There was no way in hell she was going to let Grady make the same mistake Mitch had made eight years ago. Even if she had to lose a friend over it.

This time Alex would do whatever it took.

_11_

AFTER MAKING LOVE till the wee hours last night, and a lazy Sunday morning in bed, Lily couldn't help a twinge of depression. Tomorrow Ethan would be at work. And she had to be at the spa at the Monte Carlo Resort and Casino bright and early. She wasn't looking forward to it.

The past couple of days had been maybe the happiest of her life. How wonderful it had been this weekend to see Ethan loosen up and have fun. His aura was light green; his sacral chakra was completely unblocked. She'd felt more fulfilled, more…right with the universe than ever before. Her work here was almost done.

But she still had one more chakra to open.

To that end, she'd planned a special evening. She'd been waiting for just the right time for this.

She couldn't move into his place now. For one thing, he didn't need her in the same way anymore. And shifting all her pets again, just to move them out in another few days, would be too upsetting for them—Sunny had found her an apartment, and Lily was moving there next week.

That didn't mean she couldn't see him in the evenings after work for now.

She heard Ethan coming in, and checked his bedroom to make sure all was ready.

"Lily?" he called. He'd been for a run after the sun set.

"Back here," she answered, even as she heard him coming down the hall.

He poked his head in the bedroom. "I'm going to hit the show—"

An ache throbbed sharp and low between her thighs at the look in his eyes as he took in the room lit only with candles, and then landed his gaze on her. She was nude but for a red, lacy teddy. Sounds of ocean waves crashing to shore played on speakers she'd bought for her iPod.

He stepped inside as if irresistibly drawn, and she felt breathless, nervous. After all the times they'd made love. "Strip down to whatever you're comfortable in."

Within seconds he'd stepped out of his running shoes and yanked off his T-shirt, shorts and briefs. Mmm, a naked Ethan. Her passage was already wet.

With an evocative smile, she took his hand and guided him to lie on his stomach on the sheet she'd spread on the bed, his head at the end. She took a moment to admire his broad shoulders and slim waist, his taut buttocks and thick thighs before she poured the coconut oil into her palms and warmed it between them.

"Close your eyes and take in a deep breath." As he complied, she climbed on the bed and straddled his waist. "When you exhale, release all your negative thoughts." Beginning at his trapezii, she kneaded her thumbs into the thick neck muscles.

He groaned. "Mmm, that feels good."

"Shh. You're supposed to be clearing your mind of all thought." She continued to massage his traps for a few minutes more, and then moved down to his lats.

"I thought I was supposed to be releasing negative thoughts," he mumbled into the mattress. His lips were curved in a smile.

She reached back and swatted his very adorable gluteus maximus. "Quiet."

He chuckled and she stilled her hands, soaking up the sound for future playback.

"You know..." He opened his eyes and rolled his upper body to look at her. "I don't think I have any negative energy to release." The emotion in his eyes, the expression on his face pierced her heart. Why did the thought of leaving him hurt so badly?

Before, whenever she helped someone, she knew in her gut when the time was right to say goodbye and let the people she'd helped go, to be strong on their own. If Lily stayed too long, she became their crutch. Hobbling them, undermining their confidence to live their lives without her.

Giving him a mock scowl, she shook her head. "Are you going to be still and let me massage you, or not?"

She pushed him down and he obediently laid his head back on his arms.

"All right." He closed his eyes, took a deep breath and exhaled with a sigh. "Do your worst, Zen Master."

"Feel your solar plexus relaxed and calm. Your energy free of blockage."

She moved up and worked on his delts, and down his arms to his triceps, then over the obliques at his waist. So much strength in these muscles. So much smooth, warm skin to caress and enjoy. She could enjoy this body for a long time. Scooting down to sit on his calves, she massaged his glutes, and then moved to his inner thigh and his groin muscles.

Ethan groaned and, despite her weight on his calf, bent one knee. Unable to resist, she reached beneath him and stroked him.

"Lily." Rolling to his back, he sat up and reached for her, but she leaned away and grabbed the bottle of oil.

"Let me finish." Her voice was more breath than sound, but it stopped him. He slowly lay back, his abs straining, and clasped his hands behind his head.

Pouring the oil into her palms, she climbed over him, straddling him just below his erection, and began working his pecs. She avoided his eyes, but she could feel his gaze on her. He brought his hand from behind his head, reached up and brushed his knuckles over her nipple through the satin teddy. Already puckered, her nipple tightened more.

She closed her eyes, distracted, and he took advantage

and brought his other hand up to play with her neglected nipple. Aching desire raced along her nerves.

His hands slid up to drag the spaghetti straps off her shoulders, and the teddy fell to her waist. He cupped her nape and pulled her down to his mouth. "Don't ask me to wait," he mumbled against her lips, then kissed her, long, deep and greedily.

Heat spread through her body, along with a pang of soul-deep yearning she couldn't identify and decided to ignore. Much easier to concentrate on his tongue possessing her mouth and the warm oil coating her as she rubbed her breasts against his chest.

His mouth went away and she whimpered, but only as long as it took for him to roll on protection. Then he returned to take her lips once more as he gripped her waist with both hands and lifted her onto him.

Her arms around his neck, fingers clenched in his hair, she rocked in his lap while he held her tight and used his wicked lips and tongue to tame her mouth into submission.

When he shuddered against her, she moved over him faster, already on the edge, and came with him, squeezing him tight in her arms, trying to capture the moment to remember forever.

She lay on top of him, boneless, content.

"Lily?"

"Mmm?"

"This time with you has been…" He ran a hand through his hair. "I haven't lived life like this before."

"Like what?" She smiled and a lump formed in her throat at the same time.

"Like you do. Full speed. You're like an F-16 blazing through the sky."

She raised her head and looked at him. "Full of passion, you mean?"

"Yes."

"I think you have that much passion and more, bottled up inside you. You just needed someone to help you unleash it." Her stomach growled so loudly their neighbors could probably hear it.

He grinned and swatted her butt. "I think I need to feed you."

She wanted a veggie pizza, and he wanted a shower.

The delivery boy showed up while Ethan was still toweling dry. Lily's purse was, of course, in her car. Not that he ever let her pay for anything, anyway. "Grab some money out of my wallet," he yelled from the bathroom.

She shrugged into her robe, then took his wallet off the dresser, opening the black trifold as she headed to the front door. As she was pulling out some bills she noticed a tiny, battered photo tucked inside. The delivery boy had to clear his throat before she paid him.

Forgetting the pizza, she set it on the bar and studied the picture. It was of a smiling young girl, maybe six or seven years old, with the same gray-green eyes and dark hair as Ethan. From her outfit and hairstyle the picture looked to have been taken sometime in the eighties. Maybe twenty-five years ago?

Unrelenting grief swept over Lily as she stared into the girl's eyes. The emotion was so strong Lily clutched her stomach. Just as she'd felt the lingering pain in that shopping center. This was it. Whatever was blocking his heart chakra had to do with this girl. Lily's eyes filled with tears.

As if she'd conjured him up, Ethan was behind her, wrapping her in the dependable comfort of his arms.

"What was her name?" she asked softly.

"Annie." His voice was gruff. He cleared his throat.

"Your sister?"

She felt him nod against her temple. "She had leukemia." There was no emotion in his voice. As if he was speaking of a stranger. Grief wasn't an alien feeling to him. He'd spoken of losing friends in battle. And it *had* been a long time ago. But still… To lose a sibling. A sweet young girl.

"Ethan, I'm so sorry."

He nodded again.

Lily closed her eyes and ran her fingers over the photo. "Her energy isn't here, Ethan. Wherever she's gone, she's at peace." She turned in his arms. "But you're not. Why?"

He stiffened and shrugged, but she could tell he was holding in a raw pain. "It's not something I talk about."

"And that's worked for you, has it? Ignore the pain

and it will go away eventually?" She cupped his cheek and made him look at her. "If it hasn't in more than twenty-five years, I don't think it's going to."

"Men don't talk about that kind of thing," he said through gritted teeth. But his eyes were full of unshed tears.

"Why? Because it's not manly to show your feelings?" She gave him a small smile. "Will they revoke your man card if you allow yourself to grieve?"

He huffed a laugh that turned into a gulp. "According to my father, yes." Ethan's jaw was tight and his chest rose and fell as he took several deep breaths.

"She was always so happy," he whispered. "Even when she was really sick, she always made me laugh. I tried to bargain with God to take me instead." He tightened his hold on Lily. "It should have been me."

"No. Annie would want you to be at peace and appreciate living, Ethan."

He shook his head and his body trembled until finally Lily felt the air whoosh from his lungs.

And with that she sensed Ethan's chi take on a serenity she'd never felt in him before.

This was what she'd been striving for. What she'd hoped to achieve when she first met him. She'd sensed from the beginning he needed to purge the restraints he'd put on himself. To release the strictures of a lifetime.

She pulled back and smiled up at him. "No one's knocked down the door and demanded your man card back."

He chuckled and wiped his eye with the heel of his

hand. "Guess I'm safe for now." He looked down at her and she felt a wave of love and happiness emanating from him.

Lily's mind wandered. She sensed her work was done here. That she would need to leave soon. To open herself and her life to helping someone else.

But right now Ethan felt like more than just a project to her. Maybe it was just this special connection she felt after sharing his grief.

Still, the thought that soon she'd no longer be a part of his life brought a soul-crushing sadness to her heart.

He didn't need her anymore.

At that thought, her chest literally hurt. Which was ridiculous. Ethan had let go of years of grief and guilt, but…the sense of peace and satisfaction she usually felt after helping someone just wasn't inside her. Her chi was a jumbled mess.

WHEN HIS ALARM WENT OFF, Ethan slammed his palm on the snooze button and then rolled back over to throw his arm around Lily. He pushed his erection into her bottom and played with her breast, but she only elbowed him away and kept sleeping. He chuckled. He'd learned this past weekend that she wasn't exactly a morning person.

Climbing out from between the sheets, he gave Lily's nude body a long, leisurely perusal, then smiled and stretched before making his way to the shower.

The fact that he found himself smiling so often was just one of the things he couldn't quite get used to.

Two weeks ago he'd never have imagined there might be more to life than his career. He'd started working when he was fourteen, and he'd been employed ever since. But he'd discovered he liked having time for fun. And not only that, he'd begun thinking he deserved it.

Lily had turned his life upside down. And the crazy thing was, he was happy.

He'd never had a woman like Lily in his life. And he wanted to explore the relationship.

Now he knew how Jackson felt.

At the time, he'd thought his buddy was crazy to give up his career and move in with a girl after knowing her only a few short weeks. But Jackson had been in lo—

Damn. Was he in love?

Ethan thought back to last night and the surge of unnamed emotion he'd felt for Lily after talking about Annie. The weight that had been lifted. Was it more than gratitude?

Before he left, he bent over to the bed and kissed Lily's cheek, then stood staring at her again. He pictured how sweet the lovemaking had been last night. And after, he'd still wanted to hold her. Was that love?

What would it be like to wake up next to her every day? Not just until she got her own place, but...forever.

If things worked out.

As he drove into Nellis, he decided to speak to the commander about more PTO. Spending a few weeks with her on a warm beach under some palm trees didn't sound too awful.

Once he got to his office the first thing he did was look at his calendar. He made a note to check with his squadron commander, and then headed out for his first class of the day.

At lunch he thought about calling Lily to see how her day was going, but as he grabbed a tray in the commissary, Hughes and McCabe waved him over to their table.

Hughes had apologized to Lily Saturday night, or Ethan might not have joined them. "Hotter than hell out today," he said as he took a seat across from them.

McCabe nodded and grinned. "The hotter the weather, the skimpier the women's clothes."

"Ugh, McCabe." Hughes rolled her eyes and set her sandwich down.

"I'm thinking a beach somewhere would be nice. Somewhere private where Lily and I can lie around and get to know each other better."

"Ahh, maybe a nude beach," McCabe teased.

Ethan scoffed. "No one's going to see Lily nude but me."

Hughes avoided his eyes, her mouth shut tight. She was tapping the toe of her boot.

McCabe jumped into the silence. "I haven't got much time off left. Used a week when Jackson got to town. And then a few days when he was in the hospital. Probably wait."

"Good, 'cause I think I'll take Lily to—"

"Sir, come on." Hughes flattened her hands on the

table and pierced him with a fiery gaze. "You can't be serious about that girl."

Ethan gritted his teeth. "What's your problem, Hughes?"

She blinked and curled her hands into fists. "You have to understand. I said nothing while McCabe made a huge mistake and…I wish like hell I'd stopped him. I just don't want to see you get hurt."

"She may be a little out there with some of her 'I see auras' stuff. But I don't take it all that seriously."

"It's not that." Hughes dropped her gaze. "Maybe she told you. Maybe y'all worked it out. Maybe I'm talking out of my ass."

An icy chill shot down Ethan's spine. "Spit it out, Hughes. Told me what?"

She looked back up at him, her expression bleak. "That night at the banquet. Lily talked about helping you, remember?"

"Yeah, she said that when I first met her, too. I told you, she's a little out there."

"After you left…later, she was talking to Mitch. She said she'd helped lots of guys, and that as soon as she helped you it'd be time to move on. Like you were just another poor schmuck who needed her special talents."

The ice spread into Ethan's veins, circulated through his lungs and into his heart. His chest hurt, the pain sharp and stabbing. He felt frozen. Couldn't move. Not even his jaw, or his tongue. No words made sense. No action seemed to matter.

"Sir? Grady? Are you all right?"

Hughes's voice seemed faraway. It was a fly he wanted to swat. But he couldn't move.

"Grady. Maybe I'm wrong. Maybe she felt that way at first, but she's changed now. Maybe—"

"I'm fine, Hughes," he interrupted. "This thing with Lily was always temporary. We're just having fun." *Fun.* His gut wrenched. "Now if you'll excuse me, I have sorties."

Ethan tried to smile as he got up, but he wasn't sure it was successful. At least he made it out of the commissary and back to his office before he started to shake.

12

SOMETHING WAS TERRIBLY wrong.

Ethan's place was dark, the blinds drawn against the late-afternoon heat. But he hadn't turned any lights on. When he'd called the Monte Carlo and asked her to come over right after work, his voice had been as cold as the arctic.

"Ethan?"

"Here."

Lily jumped. He was sitting on the sofa, so still she hadn't noticed him there. "What are you doing?" Her uniform itched and smelled, and she desperately wanted to shower and change.

He didn't answer, didn't even turn to look at her.

"Ethan?"

"What am I to you, Lily?"

"What?"

"You heard me."

Instead of heading to the bathroom, she kicked off

her shoes and sat beside him on the sofa, tucking her legs beneath her. "Ethan, your aura—"

"I don't want to hear about my aura. Just answer the question."

"What's happened? Why are you so angry?"

"Goddamn it, Lily." She flinched as his nostrils flared, and the muscle in his jaw ticked. "I've been trying to remember what you said the night we met. After the fire. You said it was karma. And that you could help me with my chi."

"Yes."

"And that stuff at the banquet. About my chakra."

She nodded. "Yes?"

He finally turned his head to look at her. "So, is that all I am to you? A project? Someone to *fix?*" His face was a mask. Cold steel. Except for that jaw muscle. "And am I cured now? Are you ready to move on to the next poor schmuck?"

His anguish was clear. Seeking to soothe him, she cupped his jaw in her palm. "I'm your friend. And I hope we can always be friends."

He pushed her hand away and shoved himself off the sofa. "Friends? I already have friends." Scrubbing his hand across his jaw, he strode to the kitchen and pulled the pitcher of water from the fridge. "I'll be going out of town for a while. So don't move back here."

"Ethan." She stood and followed him into the kitchen. "We've had fun, haven't we? Let's not ruin what we have."

"Fun?" His look of rage pinned her in place.

Hatred. Pain. Fear. So much negative energy. She could feel the choking black clouds creeping into her chi. It hurt to think she was the cause. What had she done?

She needed to calm her racing pulse and roiling stomach so she could think straight. She squeezed her eyes shut and pressed her fingers to her temples. "I can't do this right now. Can we talk about it later?"

"There's nothing to talk about." He pushed past her to the condo door. "You're right. It's been fun." He opened it and waited expectantly.

Lily had no idea how to respond. The headache spiked from her temples to behind her eyes. She moved to the door, but paused beside him. He was so hurt, and it was her fault. She'd made a mess of things. She could only hope she hadn't undone everything she'd tried to do for him.

She reached up on her tiptoes to kiss him, but he jerked his face away. "Goodbye, Lily."

It would be all right. Wouldn't it? Ethan would come to accept that it had to be this way. "Goodbye, Ethan."

The door slammed shut behind her and Lily started shaking. A silent sob escaped. She wanted to turn around and pound on the panel until he let her in.

And say what?

What did he want from her? Love? He'd never mentioned love. She'd felt it pouring from him the night he'd talked about Annie. But that had been for his sister, hadn't it? But could Lily commit to loving only one person the rest of her life? She loved everyone karma sent into her path, but romantic love never lasted. Just look at her mother's messed up relationships over the years. And what about Theo? She'd never been able to love him back the way he wanted her to. Or any one guy, for that matter. There was so much negativity in the expectation of romantic love. She'd come to believe her gift had rendered her incapable of giving her whole heart.

Why couldn't friendship have been enough for Ethan? She didn't like ending things this way. It hurt so much. She ran to The Pumpkin and plopped inside. Then let the torrent of tears come.

HEAVING EXHAUSTED BREATHS, Ethan used his teeth to peel loose the Velcro and slip off his boxing gloves. He'd punched the bag until he couldn't hold his arms up anymore. And he still felt like beating something to a bloody pulp.

He bent over, bracing his hands on his knees, trying to keep his mind blank. Then he caught the glint of something shiny on the floor beside the futon. He looked closer. A condom packet. A deluge of memories sent him out the door and jogging down to the running path. Each time his right foot hit pavement the word *fool* sounded in his head with a steady rhythm. *Fool. Fool. Fool.*

He'd been willing to change his life for her. And she had thought they were just friends. Some psychic she was.

As he rounded a curve in the running path, he silently

thanked Alex for the truth. How much worse it would have been if he'd come home ignorant of the facts and told Lily of his plans to take a vacation with her. Or, God forbid, if he'd told her he loved her.

How could he have been so duped? He'd always prided himself on being a good judge of character. He squeezed his eyes shut and tried to force out images of long, strawberry curls wrapped around his fingers, and big blue eyes smiling up at him, and those dimples...

He had to stop thinking about her. His chest literally hurt when he did. And he couldn't stand this heartache, couldn't sustain this level of pain for as long as it might take to get over her. No wonder McCabe drank. He'd actually married a woman before he found out she didn't love him.

A finger or two of Scotch sounded good right about now. Ethan almost pulled out his cell to call McCabe to meet him at Duffy's. But getting drunk would be only a temporary fix. He needed something more permanent to take his mind off Lily. Something else on which to focus his attention. And get him away from his condo with all its memories. Hell, away from Vegas would be better.

And the only thing he could think of that would take every bit of his concentration, and energy, and that would get him far enough away...was combat.

THREE WEEKS LATER, Ethan pulled his SUV out through the gates at Nellis and headed for home, maybe for the last time. He'd decided to list his condo with a real estate agent. It was a bad market for selling right now, but he didn't give a goddamn. He'd find something new once his combat tour was up. Assuming he was even stationed at Nellis again.

He was merging onto the highway when the car behind him sped up and pulled around him, and the car behind that...was an orange Toyota with a redhead behind the wheel.

What the—? Was she stalking him? She'd left several messages on his cell saying she needed to talk to him, but he figured if he ignored her, she'd get the hint. He took the next exit and pulled into a gas station. She followed. What did she want? He got out and faced her.

"Ethan." She jumped out of her car and stalked over to him. She was wearing her Monte Carlo uniform.

He folded his arms and leaned against his door, striving for a casualness he didn't feel. "What do you think you're doing?"

"You wouldn't return my calls. I didn't know how else to talk to you." She looked tired. There were dark circles under her eyes. Damn it. He missed her.

"We have nothing left to say." He didn't want to be this close to her. Smell her perfume. See her freckles.

"Did you really volunteer for combat?"

He narrowed his eyes. "Who told you that?"

"Mitch."

Damn it. McCabe should mind his own damn business.

"So it's true? But why would you do that?"

Ethan shrugged. "The president needs air combat

instructors in Iraq." *And I can't be in the same town with you right now.*

She chewed on her bottom lip. "Can you tell them you changed your mind?"

He snorted. "Yeah, I'll do that."

"Ethan, please don't go." He'd never seen her look so seriously worried. "Something awful will happen to you if you go over there. I know it sounds crazy, but I just know it will."

He shook his head. Lily and her crazy *feelings.* "I was fighting in the Middle East when you were still in kindergarten." He shoved off the car door and pulled the handle to open it.

"Wait." She grabbed his wrist. "I had this same feeling about Theo. Before he was deployed. I knew something bad would happen, but he wouldn't believe me." Her eyes filled with tears. "His Humvee was blown up six months after he got to Iraq."

A rush of longing swamped Ethan—a desire to hold her in his arms and comfort her. "People die in war, Lily. There's nothing you could have done." He gently pulled his wrist from her grasp.

She dropped her gaze to the ground. "But he wouldn't have enlisted if I'd loved him the way he wanted me to. And now you." Her voice had become a whisper.

Ethan sighed. He sure as hell didn't need her pity. "Listen to me." He bent his knuckle under her chin and made her look at him. "I'm not going into combat. I'm just going to train Iraqis to fly, okay? I won't be in any direct danger."

She shook her head, a tear spilling onto her cheek. "You will. Something bad will happen."

"Lily, that's just your guilt talking. No need. I'm good. I misread the cues. It wasn't your fault."

She stared at him. "You don't believe me, either." Her chin rose and her shoulders straightened, but the fear didn't leave her eyes. "Okay," she said, nodding in acceptance. "I don't know how to describe it. It's not like a dream where I can see what happens." She fished a tissue from her uniform pocket and dabbed at her nose. "I just get a feeling. And sometimes one of the four elements comes into it. You've had fire and water in your life recently. It's either air or the earth. Maybe both. I think it has something to do with the earth." She closed her eyes a moment, and then looked back into his. "With dirt or...soil, maybe?" She shrugged, then stepped close and clamped her arms around his middle, pressed her cheek to his chest and squeezed tight. The feel of her against him shoved the air from his lungs. He swallowed a lump in his throat.

She pushed away, rushed back to her car and drove off.

It was a good thing she'd pulled out of his arms when she did. Another few seconds and he might not have been able to let her go.

LILY LAY ON THE FLOOR of her apartment and stroked Ingrid, who was lying on top of her stomach. Mist was here, talking about something, but Lily's eyes were closed. She kept daydreaming of Ethan. But it was more like a nightmare. In it he was wearing desert camouflage. He was holding a rifle and using a bombed building for cover while he fought the Taliban. Which was ridiculous because he flew fighter jets. He didn't fight on the ground.

"So, do you think you can help him, Lil'?" Mist leaned back in her pink beanbag chair, plunking on his guitar.

She opened her eyes and saw her apartment ceiling. She'd barely gotten home from work and out of the shower when Mist rang her doorbell. He hadn't seen her new place yet.

"Lily?" He punctuated her name by strumming an off-key chord.

"I'm sorry." She rolled to her side, dislodging Ingrid, who strutted away in a tiff. "Who is this guy?" She tried to give Mist her attention this time.

"I told you. He comes into the coffeehouse all the time."

Mist played his electronic music for tips on Friday and Saturday nights at a little club close to her old shop. That's where she'd met him, years ago. Helped him through some baggage he'd had with his old man, and Lily and he had become good friends.

"—rude to the waitresses and then apologizes right away. Uh-huh. Has fangs and blue fur, oh, and he comes from outer space."

"Okay." She nodded. "Wait. What?"

Mist strummed his guitar. "Where are you, Lil'?"

Lily just wanted to cry. "I don't know. I'm sorry, what were you saying?"

"I said he lost a leg in Iraq and I'm pretty sure he's got PTSD. Thought you might want to check out his aura."

She nodded and then shook her head. "I don't think I'm ready yet, Mist, I'm sorry."

"It's been over a month. You've never taken this long to find someone to help."

"I know. I think it's the job." *Liar.* "It's just draining me, right now."

"So, you don't even want to meet him?"

"Maybe in a couple of weeks?" she said, begging off. "Just give me some more time, okay?"

Maybe by then she'd have seen a sign that Ethan was going to be okay, and that she was meant to help someone else.

Now you're lying to yourself. The truth was, she didn't want to do this anymore. She'd gotten too involved with Ethan, too emotionally connected to be objective anymore. But if she couldn't help people, then what was her life's purpose? What was she going to do?

13

ETHAN BENT LILY OVER THE BED, shucked his briefs and pushed his cock deep inside her from behind. She shouted encouragement and pushed back against him as he clutched her hips and pounded into her. He was so primed, so ready, he knew he wouldn't last, but she had to come with him. "Lily?"

She reached beneath and stroked herself. "Yes, almost... Now!"

When he heard her cry out, he thrust one more time and let go. The room circled around him as if his aircraft had fallen into a tailspin.

Ethan jerked awake.

Damn.

Even when he slept, she was there. Sometimes she was wearing the harem girl outfit, and sometimes she wore nothing except the red teddy and her sweet crooked smile. Night after night she haunted him. He still wanted her. He wanted her rough, he wanted her tender, tied up, or on top—it didn't matter. He bit back a groan. This was nothing but self-torture.

He ran a hand through his hair and checked his watch: 0410. Joints creaking, muscles sore, he rolled out of his bunk and pulled on his BDUs. Checked the boots for scorpions and grabbed a bottle of water, preparing to hit the day.

He was proud of the job he was doing here. As part of Squadron 3, he helped provide mission training to the Iraqis. It was all about helping rebuild Iraq's air force. The days were long, hot and dusty, but for the most part his life wasn't much different than Nellis except for the facilities and the nightlife. And he'd never been one for a lot of nightlife.

If he could just stop thinking about Lily. He pictured her beaming at him when he came home, feeding him strawberry shortcake, lying beside him on the shore of Lake Mojave. The hell of it was, he'd flown over seven thousand miles to get away from her, but she was still as close as the next daydream.

And worse, he kept thinking about her "bad feeling," and her warning. He'd been here five weeks and not a day had gone by that he hadn't tried to interpret her cryptic advice. The earth? He was a pilot, for chrissakes. Of course, the earth could be a bad thing. If he crashed into it.

He'd never been superstitious before. But now he found himself double-checking parachute packs and fuel tanks. And that irritated the hell out of him.

As the sun rose Ethan was on the airfield with his squadron commander and the Iraqi air force colonel, going through preflight checks before taking off. Who'd have thought he'd be flying props again? But the Cessna 208 was like the lighter C-172 on steroids. She was a nice single engine with surveillance and bombing capabilities.

Ethan trained Iraqis to fly two different missions. One for intelligence, surveillance and reconnaissance, and the other for ground attack.

Today they were going on a live fire exercise with an AGM-114 Hellfire missile. The target was a shack located on a bombing range on Al Asad Air Base 184 kilometers to the southwest. The Iraqi airmen were eager to be firing a live rocket at a target, and Ethan could feel the energy in the air.

He climbed aboard and put on his headset, letting his Iraqi trainee, Colonel Amad Bahrim, communicate with the tower, and then they were down the runway and in the air. Colonel Bahrim banked to the left and the morning sun shone directly into their eyes. Ethan smiled as the airman gave him a thumbs-up and adjusted the Randolph Aviator sunglasses Ethan had given him a day after arriving on base.

The flight proceeded without incident, and when Bahrim fired the missile and hit the target dead on, there was a lot of hooting and cheering on the airwaves.

The second plane flew recon and surveillance, recording the mission, filming the explosion and checking the damage. By the time they were done they had just enough fuel to return to Kirkuk.

They were approximately thirty kilometers from Baghdad when Ethan spotted something strange on the horizon. It looked like a patch of orange fog in the blue sky.

Colonel Bahrim said something about Allah. And not in a good way.

"What is it?" Ethan looked at him and back at the fog. It was growing by the second.

"Sandstorm," Bahrim whispered, terror in his voice.

Ethan cursed long and loud. He'd heard reports of last year's storm. It had lasted a week and reached all the way from Kirkuk in the north to Kuwait and the Gulf. Practically the entire country had been shut down. And hundreds had been killed.

If that kind of sand got in the Cessna's engine they were doomed. Their only chance was to outrun it. And if it was as big as last year's, it wouldn't matter where they flew. But one thing was for sure—they needed to turn the hell around and get this plane on the ground.

Adrenaline kicked in and Ethan's pulse raced. "Colonel, I'll take the controls. We might have to land suddenly. You radio back to Rodriquez and warn them we're turning. Then get ahold of the tower in Baghdad. See if they have any information on the storm, and then ask about landing strips to the east."

Bahrim nodded and Ethan banked the plane to the

right. He began checking his speed and calculating their fuel level and how far they could go at full throttle.

When the colonel couldn't reach the Baghdad tower, Ethan swore. Not good. The storm had already reached the capital and cut off communications. It was big, it was traveling fast, and they were on their own finding a landing strip—a choice between bad and worse. Land sooner on the flattest surface they could find before the storm overtook them, or fly as far as they could to find a proper landing strip. Either way, they could be trapped inside the Cessna for days.

Ethan chose to look for a landing strip. A bad landing had the potential for more injuries, and if the storm started catching up, he could hunt for a road then.

"Colonel Bahrim, see if there's a map of Iraq. We need a landing strip. But a road will do."

"Only one road directly to the east, Lieutenant Colonel Grady. The road to Ar Rutbah."

Ethan grimaced, his stomach churning. "Then that's where we head."

They'd flown only twenty kilometers when what looked like a solid wall of sand stretching from horizon to horizon started catching up to them. This was it. If they waited any longer, they'd be landing with no engine. Ethan banked to the right and dropped altitude, looking for the road. A light dusting of sand was already hitting the windshield when he put her down on it, praying there wasn't any oncoming traffic.

Watching the giant wall of sand rushing toward them, he braced for impact. With the force of a tidal wave the rolling cloud of orange hit the plane and flipped her over and over. His seat belt helped, but the sand and wind were too powerful, the storm too massive. The world outside spun.

Ethan's right leg twisted and he heard it snap. His head hit the door and cracked the glass, and the cockpit became a jumble of flashing pictures. His skull was pounding and his hands shook. Blood was dripping from his temple into his eye. Just before he lost consciousness he thought of Lily.

He wanted to see her again one more time. He wanted a chance to tell her she'd been right. He should have believed in her. The earth had risen up into the air in dirt and dust and sand, and caused something bad to happen.

And he wished he'd kissed her one more time.

ANOTHER LONG DAY AT THE spa. But then, every day seemed endless since things had ended so badly with Ethan. In the five weeks since he'd left, the bad feeling about him had only gotten worse. Her chi was all messed up. Completely out of balance. She couldn't meditate and she couldn't sleep.

Lily trudged out to the employees' parking area, climbed into The Pumpkin and turned on the radio.

The new age music helped relax her. Halfway home, the DJ broke in with a special news report. A massive sandstorm had hit Iraq. Lily froze.

Earth. Dirt. *Sand*.

She didn't even know where in Iraq Ethan was

stationed. If he'd been flying at the time... She listened raptly for details.

The news report said the storm could last for days, maybe as long as a week. Towns were buried, planes were down all over the country and several aircraft were missing. But of course they weren't releasing any names. They couldn't send out search and rescue teams until the storm passed. Then the radio went to a commercial break.

Lily's hands were trembling, but she made herself stay calm until she made it to her new apartment. She stripped out of her uniform and showered.

The rest of the evening her stomach was queasy. As she took care of her pets and tried to choke down a can of soup, she remembered sitting at Theo's funeral five years ago and accepting the flag the army men folded off his coffin. If Ethan was killed, she wouldn't even have that right. She was nothing to him. But he was all she could think about.

She couldn't bear to think she might never see him again. Hold him again. She didn't remember feeling that way about Theo after he'd died. She'd mourned him. But she hadn't wanted to curl up in bed and disengage from life. And she'd known they would notify her if something happened. She had no way of knowing if Ethan...

A sob escaped and she gave up. She had to do something. She had to find out if he was all right.

After explaining the situation to her boss the next morning, she left the Monte Carlo at lunchtime and headed to Nellis. At the gate, she asked to speak to Captain Mitch McCabe or Captain Alex Hughes. Then she waited. And waited.

She paced the front gate. She tried making small talk with the guard, but he wouldn't or couldn't carry on a conversation.

His aura was muddy and she might normally have questioned the cause, but all her thoughts were focused on one man.

Finally, about two o'clock, a shiny new Jeep pulled up inside the gate and parked by the guardhouse. It was Mitch, in a flight suit and mirrored sunglasses. He slammed his door and strode up to talk to the guard. After a moment of them glancing at her as they spoke, the guard opened the gate and Mitch approached her.

"What do you want?"

Lily couldn't see his eyes behind the mirrored glasses, but his aura was still red, and his tone was hostile. Not unexpected.

"I don't blame you for being angry with me, but I need to know if you've heard from Ethan. Is he okay?"

Mitch's lips tightened. "Don't see that Grady is any business of yours."

She stood her ground. "I know you don't believe me. But I…" She swallowed painfully. "I care about him. Please."

He crossed his arms over his chest, lowered his head and cursed under his breath. When he looked up, he took off his sunglasses. His eyes were red, as if he hadn't slept well in a while. She knew the feeling.

"He left the air base at Kirkuk yesterday morning on a training mission. His last communication was somewhere over Al Asad Air Base a few hours later. That was just before the storm hit Al Asad."

Lily rolled her lips inside her mouth to keep them from trembling, but she couldn't stop her eyes from tearing up.

Turning his head, Mitch frowned and his jaw tightened. "Grady's one of the best pilots I know. I'm sure he's fine. The storm's just knocked out communications right now."

She nodded, took a deep, calming breath and wiped her cheeks. "Thank you for telling me. Could I ask one more favor? When you hear any more news, would you call me?" She dug in her purse for her new business card and a pen, and wrote her cell number on the back. "Anytime, day or night. I just need to know."

How long a few seconds could seem when one was waiting for a life-altering decision. Mitch didn't acknowledge the card. He scrutinized Lily with suspicious eyes. "You tell me one thing first. Why would you do that to a guy?"

"I…" How to explain. "I thought I could help him."

McCabe shook his head. "Help him? By making him think you loved him?"

"I didn't— It's just that his aura was so black. I thought if I could only help him unblock his chakras and fix his—"

"Right." Mitch snorted. "You wanted to change him. What is it with you women, always trying to fix a man?

You either love him the way he is or leave him the hell alone."

His words echoed in her head. *Always trying to fix a man. Fix him.* Ethan had asked her if he was just someone to fix.…

Lily's paradigm shifted. She'd offered change. What she thought of as enlightenment. But maybe enlightenment wasn't always about trying to change someone else. Maybe it was about her accepting someone just as he was.

Ethan's dark emotions and intense nature were a part of him. He didn't need to change. Or be *fixed*. He just needed to be loved for who he was. He needed…someone to love him for the man he already was.

The realization made her head pound. She rubbed her temples, trying to alleviate the sharp pressure, but more tears welled up and she squeezed her eyes shut. *She loved him.*

That's why she couldn't help anyone else. Why she was a basket case all the time now.

She'd been so blind. From the moment she'd met Ethan, he'd felt different. She'd passed off that special link as just energies connecting. But she'd been too afraid to believe in her love. Afraid of getting hurt, like her mom and Theo had been hurt. Afraid she couldn't give him what he needed most.

Please let him be alive. Please.

Lily closed the distance between her and Mitch. "You're right. I was an idiot. I shouldn't have tried to change Ethan. But I do love him. Just the way he is."

And she wanted a chance to tell him that she was ready to risk opening her heart to him. She wished she could be with him. But even if she knew where he was, or could reach him, would he want her there? Could he forgive her?

"Please, Mitch. I just need to know if he's okay. I love him. All I want is a chance to tell him how wrong I was."

The airman hesitated, searching her face with narrowed eyes. With a resigned sigh, he took her card. "Man, I must be the biggest sucker born."

Overwhelmed with gratitude, Lily hugged him. "Thank you."

He stood stiff in her arms, and she let go and backed off.

Raising a brow, Mitch nodded and returned to his car. His agreement to notify her of Ethan's status was all she could ask.

It would be enough. For now.

SIX DAYS LATER Lily had her answer when her cell phone rang. "Hello?"

"Lily, this is Mitch McCabe."

"Yes? Is he okay?" It was the worst second of her life. She squeezed her eyes closed. "Please tell me he's alive."

"He's in critical condition. When they found him he'd lost a lot of blood."

But he was alive. There was hope. "Where is he? Can I go see him?"

"No. He's in Germany. If I learn anything new, I'll let you know." He ended the call.

All Lily could do was wait. And hope.

But he was alive.

14

ETHAN SMELLED disinfectant. And he heard voices, but he couldn't understand what they were saying. He didn't want to open his eyes, but a female voice kept badgering him, calling his name.

She was here. She'd come to see him. God, he'd missed her. "Lily?" He opened his eyes. The face leaning over him was blurry. But he could tell it wasn't Lily.

"Well, welcome back. Can you tell me your name?"

Ethan blinked a couple times and the figure in front of him cleared. Intelligent brown eyes in a caramel-toned face with an inquiring expression. She was dressed in blue scrubs and held a clipboard stuffed with papers.

"Sir? Can you tell me your name?" She'd spaced each word out as if he couldn't understand English.

He scowled. "You were just calling my name over and over." His voice was nothing but a croak. "You forgot it already?"

Her brows raised in an oh-no-you-didn't look. "Why

don't you humor me, flyboy. Unless you'd like an enema today?"

"Lieutenant Colonel Ethan Grady, 414th Combat Training Squadron."

"Mmm-hmm. That's what I thought." She handed him a cup of water with a straw. "I'm Dr. Williams."

He didn't do straws. He tried to sit up, but that wasn't happening.

"Whoa. Hold on, now." The doctor gently stilled him. "You've been out for a while. You're going to have to take it easy."

"How long?" He turned his head to look for a window. It was weird as hell not to know if it was night or day, or even what day it was.

"Four days since you came here. Two days missing before that. You're at Landstuhl. You suffered a concussion, six broken ribs and a compound fracture of your right tibia."

He looked down at his body, clenched his fists and wiggled his toes. All present and accounted for. "Is everything there under that cast?"

"You're lucky. You still got your leg. What do you remember?"

The storm, landing, hitting his head. When he woke up— "Colonel Bahrim. The other man in the plane with me. Is he…?"

Her face softened into a wide smile. "He's just fine, sir. Beat up and bruised like you, but he'll be good to go in no time."

Something eased inside Ethan. "Thank you."

She turned to leave.

"Doc?"

She swiveled back around. "Yes, Lieutenant Colonel?"

"When can I get out of here?"

She put her hand on her hip and raised one brow. "Was it something I said? Maybe two weeks. We'll see how fast you get better."

Within two weeks he was stable enough to travel with crutches. They told him his right leg might need another surgery once he got back to the States. But for Ethan, getting home couldn't happen fast enough.

He landed at Andrews, and saw a doctor at Walter Reed. The doc put him on official medical leave until such time as he was cleared for flight duties. Then Ethan was sent home to Nellis. He knew he was one lucky son of a gun, and he wanted to go back and finish his tour, but damn he was glad to be back in the City of Sin.

When he'd woken up in that sand-covered plane, his first thought was he had to get back to Lily. His second was that he needed psychiatric treatment. She didn't want him.

But the yearning to see her one more time, to hold her once more made him crawl out with his useless leg, even though his chest felt as if it was on fire with each move, and wave his undershirt until the search and rescue helicopter team saw him.

And the hell of it was, when McCabe and Hughes met him at the airport he still wanted to ask about her.

"Grady, you dog!" McCabe gave him a one-armed hug.

Ethan winced. For fear of pneumonia, the doctors hadn't wrapped his ribs.

"Welcome home, sir." Hughes saluted, and then crammed her hands in her pockets. Her eyes looked moist. *Aw, damn.*

"Captain Hughes. You mind getting my kit?" Ethan gestured with a crutch to his duffel. Normally, he hated like hell asking for help, but Hughes needed something to do.

"Yes, sir." She grinned and grabbed it.

On the way home, they picked up some barbecue and caught him up on all the news from Nellis. He'd been gone only nine weeks, but it seemed like years. At his condo—still unsold—they helped him unpack, but he guessed they could see the flight had taken its toll. They shook his hand and left him to rest.

Grady dropped to his soft leather sofa to ease the throbbing in his leg. It had been a long four weeks since the storm, but he was finally home.

Alone. He looked around at his bare and boring rooms. No color. No life. No Lily.

Every moment he'd spent with her came rushing back and hit him like that wall of sand. He was tumbling in memories. The animals, the plants. Her.

Lily practicing yoga naked. Offering him strawberry shortcake. Playing with pet toys and prattling about any and everything. Beneath him on the futon, her breasts filling his palms. Above him, her soft hair brushing his skin. He closed his eyes and groaned. He missed her.

Deep inside, way beneath the broken ribs, his chest felt vacant.

He wasn't sure he could go back to life as he knew it before her.

The doorbell rang. Getting his crutches under him, Ethan gimped over and opened it. "McCabe?"

The man nodded and shuffled his weight from one foot to the other. His mouth was a tight line. Finally, he drew a deep breath. "I almost didn't give you this." He pulled an envelope the size of a greeting card from his pocket. It had been folded in half, but was still sealed. "But I figure you're a grown man and you can make your own decisions." McCabe handed it to him.

Ethan read his name on the outside, written in a feminine scroll.

"She's more stubborn than I would have thought. I'll give her that."

"Thanks." Ethan extended his right hand and Mitch shook it.

"Good luck." His friend saluted, spun on his heel and headed for his Jeep.

Ethan went back to his couch and sat down, laying his crutches beside him. It seemed thick for a greeting card. Common sense told him not to open it. Why risk getting screwed over again?

Who was he kidding? He ripped the envelope.

It was one of those cards that played a song when you opened it. The front of the card said: "Without you I'm like a fish without water."

Ethan opened the card and Tim McGraw and Faith Hill were singing "I Need You."

On the inside she had crossed out the printed words and written her own.

> I need you like a candlelit room needs a fire extinguisher,
> Like a guinea pig needs a cage,
> Like a bass boat needs a fisherman.
> I'm sorry. I love you. Could I have a second chance?

Ethan's hand shook as he reread the card. A hard lump was lodged in his throat. And his jaw hurt from gritting his teeth.

Only a crazy, weird, silly person would send a card like this. He should toss it away and never look back. She was flighty. She could change her mind tomorrow. She talked too much.

But she'd been quiet when he was fishing.

She had all those animals.

But she cared for all those animals without blinking an eye.

Was he really going to do it?

IT'D BEEN OVER A WEEK since Ethan had returned to Las Vegas. Lily knew because she'd pried the information out of Mitch the second time she'd gone by the air base to ask about Ethan, by promising to never call or ask for Mitch at Nellis again.

She'd also learned he had delivered her card.

So that was it. Ethan had moved on. If he'd ever

cared for her, he didn't anymore. If he did, wouldn't he have called her before now? She'd been telling herself he probably had medical appointments. He had to rest a lot. But if there was anything she'd learned the hard way lately, it was that there came a time when a person had to face the truth.

She'd lost him.

After stuffing her purse in her locker, she left the Monte Carlo employees' lounge and headed up the elevator to the spa. The calendar was packed with clients' appointments. She had three Swedish massages, two deep tissues and one nature's essence aroma massage booked back-to-back before lunch.

She worked all morning, and was feeling the burn after the two deep tissue massages. All that was left was the aroma massage. It was a little easier on her hands.

She checked the appointment book for the client's name. *Mr. Smith?* She frowned. With no first name? With a shrug, she grabbed the client's chart out of the rack by the door and swept into the massage room. A man sat on a chair in the corner, a magazine hiding a face.

Her skin prickled.

The magazine slowly lowered and dropped to a table. Ethan reached for some crutches and got to his feet. "Lily." His face remained perfectly serious. Perfectly... perfect.

She couldn't breathe, couldn't stop blinking as tears threatened. "Ethan." She started toward him, longing to touch him. To know it was him and that he was truly okay.

There were a million things she wanted to say to him, but she couldn't conjure a single coherent thought. "I…"

He closed the distance between them, using his crutches like a pro. His leg was in a cast from just above the knee to his ankle. He was paler and thinner, but so, so handsome.

"Can't I get a massage?" He raised a brow.

"Oh. With your broken ribs still healing? I don't think that'd be a good idea."

"Lily."

She couldn't possibly touch him without completely losing control. *I need to explain, tell him how I feel.* "Besides, I don't think you could get on the table in that cast. What if you were to fall?"

"Lily."

"Oh, Ethan." She threw her arms around his neck. He grunted and grimaced, and she dropped her arms and stepped back. "Ooh, I'm sorry."

"Lily."

"Yes, Ethan?"

"I was kidding about the massage."

"Oh." She wrung her hands. "I'm not used to you making jokes."

"Well, I've changed. *You* changed me."

"But I don't want you to change. I mean, I shouldn't have tried to change you." She couldn't keep from touching his T-shirt-clad chest. Ooh, he felt so good beneath her fingers. She just wanted to soak up his heat and strength.

He frowned. "Why not?"

"Because you're a good man." Her palms skimmed over his shoulders and down to his pecs. "Loyal, and hardworking and caring—even if you do try to hide your soft side." She dropped her arms and studied her fingers. "I was so busy trying to fix everyone else I couldn't see that I'm the one who needed to change."

"You do?"

"I'm pushy and interfering and I need to stop trying to fix people."

He cocked an eyebrow. "Well, I can't argue with that, but maybe I like you that way."

"No." She shook her head and bit her lip. "I realize now." This was hard to admit. "Ethan, I'm a hypocrite. Here I was, encouraging you to feel the pain of losing your sister, but I was too scared to open up and let myself love. I wouldn't even admit that I could love someone—I mean, really love just one person—because I didn't want to risk the pain."

He set one crutch against the wall, swept his arm around her waist and pulled her close. "You're too young for me. You talk too much. And you drive me crazy." His dark expression softened. "But I'm glad you pushed your way into my life."

She finally looked up at him. "You are?" Breathing in his masculine scent, she wanted to lay her cheek against his chest and hold him tight.

He nodded. "You were right about me, you know?"

He moved his hand from her back to push loose strands of hair away from her face and cup her cheek. "I was locked away. Living a dull life. No fun. No joy. But you came along and shook me out of my boring routine."

She blinked. Just the feel of his finger brushing her skin sent tingles everywhere. Goose bumps rose on her arms and neck. "I…" She licked her lips. "I've never felt about anyone else the way I feel about you. I can't sleep. I think about you all the time. I want your happiness even if it means I'm not happy. You're not a project to me. You don't need to be fixed. You're honorable, and caring, and…and I love you."

With a groan he lowered his head and captured her lips.

Vaguely, she heard the clatter of his other crutch hitting the floor. But she ignored it. Three months since she'd seen him. Felt him. Made love with him. It seemed like forever since she'd felt his lips on hers. She combed her fingers through his hair and kissed him back, trying to pour all her love for him into her kiss.

He lifted his mouth from hers. Reaching for her hand, he brought her palm up and placed a kiss right in the center, then turned it and traced one of the lines. "Did you know you have a very deep and long love line?" He spoke without looking up.

He was tracing the wrong line, but who cared? "I do?"

"Mmm-hmm." He softly bit into the pad of flesh below her thumb and then traced another line. "And

your life line intersects with your love line right…here."
He pointed at a spot with his finger and then kissed it.

"It does?" She couldn't catch her breath.

He kissed her wrist with openmouthed, sensuous
kisses that set her skin on fire. When his lips reached
the sleeve of her uniform, he dropped both their hands
and looked at her. "You know what that means?"

"What?" She smiled.

"It means you're fated to love one person all the rest
of your life."

"I am?" If he didn't stop being so cute she was going
to cry.

He nodded. "Yep. It's karma." He framed her face
with his hands. "Lily. You took my empty, repressed life
and filled it with passion, and I don't think I can go back
to how I used to be." He kissed her, a quick meeting of
mouths. "I love you, too."

"Oh, Ethan." She slid her arms around his neck once
more, stretched up and kissed him. "I do love you," she
mumbled into his mouth.

His arms tightened around her waist, his hands slid up
her back and he deepened the kiss, sweeping his tongue
in and crushing his mouth to hers. She whimpered, longing to feel all of him against all of her. "Ethan," she
murmured between kisses.

"Hmm?" His mouth left hers to kiss down her jaw
and neck.

"You were my last appointment."

"Mmm-hmm." He brought his mouth back to hers,
his kisses growing more desperate, more frenzied.

"So let's go home."

He groaned. "Good idea." He dropped his hands from around her and fumbled for the crutch against the wall. But he had to stop kissing her when it fell to the floor, too.

He grumbled under his breath, and Lily scrambled to grab up both crutches and hand them to him.

"Lily," he said as he took them from her and set them in place under his arms.

"Yes, Ethan?"

"I'm getting a strong feeling. In order for my chakra to be completely unblocked, you're going to have to marry me." He flashed a wide smile.

He stood there grinning and Lily wrapped her arms around his waist—gently—and pressed her cheek against his chest. She tried to speak past the tears and the lump in her throat.

"Now?" he blurted. "*Now,* you suddenly have nothing to say?"

For the first time, she didn't have anything else she wanted to say. Except… She lifted her head and looked into his gray-green eyes. "I do."

Epilogue

"I NOW PRONOUNCE YOU husband and wife," the reverend said.

Ethan faced Lily, anticipating permission to kiss his bride. He lowered his head until their lips were almost touching.

"And may your paths to enlightenment be blessed by the Goddess," Sunny added.

Ethan pulled back and raised a brow at the unlikely couple officiating at his marriage.

Sunny widened her eyes and waved a hand. "Well, go on. Kiss her!"

He cupped Lily's face in his palms and did just that. The crowd around them started clapping, but the sound was soon drowned out by a loud grumbling roar that shook the ground around them. Fire exploded from the mouth of the volcano in front of The Mirage. Molten, sizzling lava poured down the side and flames flared over the mountainside, barely stopping at the AstroTurf-covered platform where they stood.

As one, McCabe, Jackson and Hughes, standing up with him in their uniforms, produced fire extinguishers and sprayed the flames closest to them.

Ethan glared at his buddies. He would never live down burning Lily's shop to the ground.

McCabe and Jackson grinned back. Hughes shrugged.

"Leave those with the gifts. We'll put them in Lily's new shop," Ethan said, then took his bride's hand and headed toward the aisle between the folding chairs full of wedding guests.

Lily smiled up at him, grabbing at a wild strawberry curl tossed by the breeze and honeyed by the setting sun. With the wreath of fresh daisies in her hair and the plunging V-necked, slim-fitting dress, she was a tantalizing concoction of innocent and seductress. She was so beautiful. All he wanted was to get her alone.

But first, the reception.

At the front row of seats, Lily paused to give her mom a brief hug while Ethan shook his commander's hand, then they continued down the aisle. Ethan stopped midstride. He blinked and looked again. "Mom?"

His mother was here. She was crying. And next to her stood his father, ramrod stiff, his hands clasped behind him.

Lily put her palm to Ethan's back and urged him forward.

Ethan didn't remember walking toward them, but suddenly he was beside his mother and she was hugging him. Slowly, he put his arms around her. He couldn't remember when he'd ever hugged his mother. He had to bend over, she was so small. And old. Her hair was mostly gray and her face was lined.

Ethan pulled away and stared at his father. "Sir."

Hugh Grady gave a curt nod. "Son." He rocked back on his heels, and the gesture was so familiar, Ethan's reaction was sharp and visceral. "I'm proud of you, son." Hugh extended a gnarled hand, rough with decades of manual labor.

A hard knot choked Ethan's throat, but he shook his father's hand.

Next to him, Lily stood waiting. *You did this?* he asked her with his eyes.

Biting her lip in that cute way she had, she nodded.

He grinned and pulled her to him, holding her tight, burying his nose in her neck until he could regain his composure.

She combed her fingers through the hair at his nape and whispered, "I invited them back for an early Christmas before you leave."

"Fine." From being married by a new age priestess and standing next to a fake volcano, to strapping his saber on over his dress uniform and watching Lily walk down the aisle, his life had become surreal, and completely out of his control. No. It had started way before that. Ethan hadn't been in charge of anything since he met Lily.

His buddies, along with three other airmen from his squadron, drew their sabers and formed an arch. He took Lily's hand and walked through, following the carpeted path to the Mirage's grand ballroom for food, dancing and wedding cake.

Once in the ballroom, events blurred together. Dinner was served. A band started playing Billy Joel's "We Didn't Start the Fire" and everyone laughed. Speeches were given, glasses raised in toasts. Ethan just wanted to be alone with Lily, but there was the first dance, the cake to be cut, the bouquet to be thrown. And all the posing for pictures.

Finally all the hoopla wound down. Ethan said his goodbyes, exhausted by the crowd, while Lily seemed to glow with energy, and hugged everyone twice. He wanted to throw her over his shoulder, haul her out of here and have her all to himself until he deployed.

But she was surrounded by their friends.

Enough.

He broke through the circle, scooped her up in his arms and told her to wave goodbye.

"Ethan!" Lily giggled as she waved over his shoulder.

"I need you now, Lily." He pushed through the double doors and headed for the bank of elevators.

"Mmm," she murmured into his neck. "It *has* been a long week, with my mother here for Thanksgiving."

"What the—" Ethan took a second look, disbelieving his own eyes.

"What is it?" Lily craned her head to see what he was watching. "Aww."

"I wondered where they'd gone."

Downstairs, in the main lobby of The Mirage,

surrounded by slot machines and bars, were Hughes and McCabe. Both still wore their dress uniforms, complete with medals, white gloves, hats and sabers. McCabe crouched, elbows on knees, talking to a group of kids, all of them enthralled with whatever he was saying. Hughes stood beside him, looking not at the kids, but at McCabe. And the expression on her face…

Ethan had never seen Mitch interact with kids before. He shook his head and resumed his course for the elevators.

"Wow, you should have seen their auras, Ethan. They were both so happy just then. Did I tell you Alex actually invited me to spend a day with her and Jordan sometime? I'm so glad we're all friends now."

"Lily?"

"Hmm?"

"I want to make a baby with you." He wasn't getting any younger. Picturing her belly round with his child made his knees weak.

"Before you leave?"

"No." He pressed the elevator button. "Yes." He gritted his teeth. "I don't know." He had only three weeks before he left for Iraq.

"Oh, Ethan." She lifted her head to look him in the eyes and combed her fingers through his hair. "You're going to come home to me in ten months alive and well. You have to believe me."

"I do."

She smiled her crooked smile and ran her finger

down his cheek and over his lips. "And then we'll begin collaborating on a most important project."

Again he felt his world spinning out of control. But he didn't mind.

"And in the meantime, I've got a shop to rebuild. Christmas with your parents. Oh, and everyone wants to go to dinner the night before you leave. I've—"

"Lily."

"—arranged for your mom and mine to have a spa day tomorrow, and then they're going to see Siegfried & Roy's Secret Garden."

"Lily!"

"Yes, Ethan?"

"Kiss me."

She did.

* * * * *

HARLEQUIN® *Blaze*

COMING NEXT MONTH

Available October 26, 2010

REQUEST YOUR FREE BOOKS!

HARLEQUIN®

Blaze

Red-hot reads!

2 FREE NOVELS
PLUS 2
FREE GIFTS!

YES! Please send me 2 FREE Harlequin® Blaze™ novels and my 2 FREE gifts (gifts are worth about $10). After receiving them, if I don't wish to receive any more books, I can return the shipping statement marked "cancel." If I don't cancel, I will receive 6 brand-new novels every month and be billed just $4.24 per book in the U.S. or $4.71 per book in Canada. That's a saving of at least 15% off the cover price. It's quite a bargain. Shipping and handling is just 50¢ per book.* I understand that accepting the 2 free books and gifts places me under no obligation to buy anything. I can always return a shipment and cancel at any time. Even if I never buy another book, the two free books and gifts are mine to keep forever.

151/351 HDN E5LS

Name		(PLEASE PRINT)	

Address			Apt. #

City		State/Prov.		Zip/Postal Code

Signature (if under 18, a parent or guardian must sign)

Mail to the **Harlequin Reader Service:**
IN U.S.A.: P.O. Box 1867, Buffalo, NY 14240-1867
IN CANADA: P.O. Box 609, Fort Erie, Ontario L2A 5X3

Not valid for current subscribers to Harlequin Blaze books.

Want to try two free books from another line?
Call 1-800-873-8635 or visit www.morefreebooks.com.

* Terms and prices subject to change without notice. Prices do not include applicable taxes. N.Y. residents add applicable sales tax. Canadian residents will be charged applicable provincial taxes and GST. Offer not valid in Quebec. This offer is limited to one order per household. All orders subject to approval. Credit or debit balances in a customer's account(s) may be offset by any other outstanding balance owed by or to the customer. Please allow 4 to 6 weeks for delivery. Offer available while quantities last.

Your Privacy: Harlequin Books is committed to protecting your privacy. Our Privacy Policy is available online at www.eHarlequin.com or upon request from the Reader Service. From time to time we make our lists of customers available to reputable third parties who may have a product or service of interest to you. If you would prefer we not share your name and address, please check here. ☐

Help us get it right—We strive for accurate, respectful and relevant communications. To clarify or modify your communication preferences, visit us at www.ReaderService.com/consumerschoice.

HB10R

*See below for a sneak peek from
our inspirational line, Love Inspired® Suspense*

*Enjoy this heart-stopping excerpt from
RUNNING BLIND
by top author Shirlee McCoy,
available November 2010!*

**The mission trip to Mexico was supposed to be an
adventure. But the thrill turns sour when Jenna Dougherty
and her roommate Magdalena are kidnapped.**

"It's okay. I'm here to help." The voice was as deep as the
darkness, but Jenna Dougherty didn't believe the lie. She
could do nothing but lie still as hands slid down her arms,
felt the rope around her wrists.

"I'm going to use a knife to cut you free, Jenna. Hold
still."

The cold blade of a knife pressed close to her head before
her gag fell away.

"I—" she started, but her mouth was dry, and she could
do nothing but suck in air.

"Shhh. Whatever needs to be said can be said when
we're out of here." Nick spoke quietly, his hand gentle on
her cheek. There and gone as he sliced through the ropes on
her wrists and ankles.

He pulled her upright. "Come on. We may be on
borrowed time."

"I can't leave my friend," Jenna rasped out.

"There's no one here. Just us."

"She has to be here." Jenna took a step away.

"There's no one here. Let's go before that changes."

"It's dark. Maybe if we find a light…"

"What did you say?"